THE

FIND

BY

DEREK JAMES

Contents

Sinea Desert, Egypt...5

It Was Going To Be A Good Day 9

Ministry Of Defense (London, England) Sunday Morning...............10

The Road To Redemption 12

A Tempest With Intention 14

A Paradigm Shift 15

This Just In..17

A Most Curious Sermon 18

Revelation..20

God Rest Ye Naval Gentlemen 22

Darkness 24

We Interrupt This Program 26

There's Something In The Water 30

Itsy Bitsy Spider..32

Central Weather Bureau - Taipei City, Taiwan 34

What Things Shall Come...36

S.S. Ariel - Southeast Of Easter Island 38

A Mother's Love...39

Apocalypsis Iesu Christi 40

A Prayer For The Dying..42

The Monster In The Mirror...43

Fright Night...48

The Sufferer's Palace...52

The Book Of Affliction..55

Premonitions 56

From Which Forth It Gushed...58

The Book Of Novus 63

A Procession Of Tears 64

Something Wicked This Way Comes 68

Revelatio - The Final Chapter 71

And On This Rock I Will Build My Church, And The Gates 73

Let Thy Fountains Be Dispersed Abroad, And Rivers Of Waters .. 76

When The Bow Breaks The Cradle Will Fall 79

The Devil And The Deep Blue Sea 82

In This House No Butterfly Shall Dwell 85

Out Of His Belly Shall Flow Rivers Of Living Water (John 7:38) .. 87

The Lord Giveth, And The Lord Taketh Away (Job 1:21) 92

Lipman's Last Stand 95

A Noble Mind No More 97

A False Balance Is Abomination To The Lord: 100

For Thee Who Taketh Thy Bone And Break It, ... 103

The Book Of Memoirs 106

The Book Of Memoirs: Christmas Eve 107

The Little Blue Pill 109

The Book Of Memoirs: Hailey's Second Birthday 110

For Mama 112

The Book Of Memoirs: The Chill Of Skutters Lake 114

Tis The Blood Of Thy Covenant Thicker Than The Water 118

The Shiny Metal Box 120

The Day Grandma Went To Heaven 124

The Chosen One 126

The Aftermath 128

With Great Rain Comes Pretty Flowers 129

"Christy, be quiet! I'm not gonna say it again! We are in church!" . . . That's the last thing I remember Mama saying before the lights went out. I was seven years old when it happened. I'm a mother now and have two beautiful little girls of my own. They are all that matter now. Every now and then the darkness creeps back into my thoughts, and in light of the unforeseen events, I sometimes wish I had never . . . *Christine quickly banishes the thought from her mind and brushes the tear from her face,* "Come on, girls! We're gonna be late for church!"

1

Sinea Desert, Egypt

"Holy Moses! Hey, Arman! I think I got somethin' here! Look at this!" Sansar proclaimed as he brushed thousands of years of dust from its ruffled spine.

"What the hell is it?"

"Beats me. Looks like some sort a novel. It's thick as a brick! Musta been some page turner!"

"Looks more like a scripture of some sort," Arman deduced inquisitively as he stroked the dust from his four-day-old gruff. "Maybe it's the primordial Good Book itself! The Book of all Books!"

"It ain't the Bible, lil' bro'. Look at the writing. It's too weird. This is somethin' else," Sansar insisted.

"Well maybe it's just how the scribes wrote back then, I mean, it's possible."

"Yeah, and maybe we been readin' the wrong book all these years. That would explain just about everything," Sansar slurred cynically, as he wedged the old bottle of tequila, the two brothers had all but polished off, back into the dirt.

He lifted the mysterious book from its dormant tomb, up to the fluttering light of his miner's cap, "And maybe it's just an oversized Christmas catalogue from some distant civilization."

"Very funny, now be careful!" Arman implored, as he lay sprawled across the floor of the catacombs the two drunken brothers painstakingly gutted for their expedition. Man, I used to love those catalogues when I was a kid, every Christmas I would check off the toys I wanted. They were like hidden treasures, those things! I always wanted . . . "

"Are you for real?" Sansar slurred through a cloud of dust. "We may have found the meaning of life, and here you are talking about a fucking Christmas catalogue."

"You started it," Arman rebutted defensively.

"I don't know. I can't make heads or tails outta this thing," Sansar uttered in frustration. "Kinda gives me the creeps though. Here, see what you make of it." Sansar tossed the alien text into Arman's lap.

"Be careful, for God's sake! And Jesus, this thing weighs a ton!" he screamed, as he thumbed through the encrypted pages to no avail.

"I don't know, I really think we got somethin here," Sansar boasted excitely. "Now put it in the damn bag and stop messing with it. You know, we been wastin' our time down here lookin' for a bag a bones, when we shoulda been searching for the Holy Scriptures or the holy fucking grail or somethin! Nobody cares about dinosaurs anymore anyway!"

"I care about you, and you're a dinosaur," Arman ribbed affectionately. Sansar was only thirty-two, five years his elder.

"Laugh it up, little brother. Laugh it up. Now get your ass outta here before I kick it out." As the two brothers stumbled out of their make shift ferret hole like two drunken monkeys, Sansar stood up and patted the dust from his camo khakis, scoured the horizon, and hacked up a generous serving of desert sand.

"Come to think it, nobody believes in the damn Bible anymore, might as well be a dinosaur," he muttered matter of factly as he spat into wind. He looked at his younger brother inquisitively, "You believe in God, don't you, my naive little brother."

The brothers were Persian by their father and Indian by their mother, but spoke with a prominent Persian tongue. Archeologists by trade, they both delved deeply into theology, but for very different reasons - Arman desperately needed to affirm his faith, while Sansar simply needed to find his. Either way, their studies proved futile and many questions remained.

"I don't know, I think so," he answered sheepishly.

"See, that's what I mean, right there! Everybody's like, 'I don't know, I think so.' Either you believe or you don't. Maybe it's just me, but if I created a race, I sure as hell wouldn't make them wonder whether or not I fucking existed. The fact that we have to question His so called "existence" is pathetic! You don't just create a race and then go play absentee landlord. You want the company but you don't want the responsibility? That's bullshit!"

"I don't know, maybe there's a reason he doesn't communicate with us."

"You see! Once again, right there! That's what I'm saying. It's dumb asses like you that got an answer for everything. Anything that don't make sense, or don't fit into the equation, you got an answer for it. If you stop to tie your shoe and evade getting hit by a bus, it's a miracle. If you don't stop to tie your shoe and get shit canned, it's God's will. Listen, if Moses parted the sea three-thousand years ago, then why the fuck can't somebody else do it!?"

"Like who? You?" Arman chuckled.

"Anybody!! Let Jerry fucking Springer part the mother fucking sea. At least it'll make the news and everyone will see it. That's all He has do to make things right, and everything would make sense. We would finally know why the fuck we're here!"

Unlike his wiry, somewhat awkward brother, Sansar was tall and lean, a strong man, both physically and mentally, but the tequila was beginning to get the best of him. He turned away to conceal the tear that streamed down his face, took a deep breath, and looked up to the sky, "I'm sorry, my brother. You know I love you. This shit just gets me riled up. Whatever man, let's get the fuck outta here. Looks like a serious storm's blowin' in."

The two brothers stood motionless, staring into the strange desert sky, "Don't like the looks of that, little brother . . . don't like the looks of that at all. They sure do get some strange cloud cover around these parts."

2

It Was Going to Be a Good Day

"Christy! C'mon, baby. We're gonna be late for church, sweetie." I always felt Mama's love, but something changed when Hailey went to heaven. I think Mama was afraid of losing another child. She has been clinging to me like lint on a sweater, and calling me baby and sweetie ever since. I was so young when it happened, but I still miss her in the pit of my stomach. I can imagine how much Mama must miss her. In a way, I was lucky I was so young; the scars never had a chance to truly latch on.

"I have your jacket, sweetie. And here, here's your hat and scarf."

Grandma made me that scarf. It was so pretty! She knew lavender was my favorite color. She said it was just the right palette for my baby blues and blonde locks. The wool was so thick and soft, but I think it was the color that made me feel warm. Mama leaned over the bannister at the top of the stairs and playfully tossed them over the edge, in the interest of saving time, of course. I graciously accepted her little game, and snatched the hat out of the air as the scarf rained down over my head in a swirling deluge of lavender. I laughed. Mama wasn't sad. It was going to be a good day.

3

Ministry of Defense
(London, England) Sunday Morning

"Would you like some tea, Dr. Lipman?" the general inquired.

"Don't mind if I do, my good sir. Don't mind if I do. And please, it's Mr. Lipman. Doctor is just so pretentious!"

Mr. Lipman bore a remarkable resemblance to Mr. Bean. He possessed a slender, non athletic chassis, and sported a sharp plaid single-breasted suit with a completely mismatched bow tie. If not for his refined English accent and captivating eloquence, he would be a dead ringer.

"I am quite intrigued by this find you speak of with such urgency, may I?"

Lipman was amongst the top three linguistic experts on the planet - an ivy leaguer with a PhD in language, specialties in evolutionary linguistics, ancient history, hieroglyphics, Latin, and theology, and a minor in chemistry to boot. His Beanish physique kept him off the football field, but he could decipher the Rosetta Stone in thirty seconds if Pat Sajack prompted him to do so. He was the guy who could clean up on Jeopardy, but had little to no interest.

"Of course, Mr. Lipman," the general conceded as he rolled his glasses from upon his buzz cut and over his nose. "Two paleontologists brought it to our attention a few days ago. I can't say they were the most credible blokes I had ever met, but they were insistent that we take a look. Perhaps I shouldn't diminish their credibility as they have made some significant finds over the years. However, we would be remiss if we did not have an extensive background check done on these two gentlemen."

"Nonsense! A find is a find! Let us have a look, shall we?" exclaimed Mr. Lipman discerningly, wiping the tea from his chin. "If you would kindly bring me the text." Two young soldiers methodically conveyed the text in a military-issue protective plexiglass casing, as it lay perched upon a black satin pillow, like that of a sacred jewel. "If you would kindly pass me my glasses." The smile on the kindly old man seemed to disappear, and was quickly replaced by utter curiosity, like that of a little boy diligently studying his insect collection. "Yes . . . yes . . . oh . . . oh my . . . dear God . . . it cannot be real. It simply cannot be real!"

4

The Road to Redemption

"Mama, the bathroom sink is leaking again!" I shouted upstairs, as I admired my new lavender scarf in the mirror.

As I coiled the sacred gift around my neck, a terrible uneasiness came over me, as if I had been granted, or perhaps cursed, with a vision of what was to come. I shrugged it off as I usually did, and hoped with all my heart I wouldn't feel it again.

"No it's not, sweetie. Now, c'mon. How many times must I tell you, baby? We're gonna be late!" Mama never did believe me.

The walk to church was a lengthy one, but ever so scenic. It was a good quarter of a mile through town before we reached the grassy hill that led down to the old rustic parish. The humble little house of worship was the town's sanctuary, and had been since Mama was a little girl. Its inherent charm and beauty graced the quaint little town of Divinity, and offered solace from the evils that be. I guess you could say it was our safe haven, "Snug as a bug in a rug", Mama would always say. We strolled through town with a spritely step, trying to make twelve o' clock mass.

Mama said hello to Mr. Walters, washing his old restored orange and brown Malibu in his driveway. He politely tipped his cap and nodded, "Mornin', ladies. Don't ya'll look pretty today."

"Why thank you, my kind sir. Why yes we do!" I replied mischievously, as Mama chuckled, never breaking pace. Mama was on the thin side with slightly graying shoulder-length dirty blonde hair. Grandma was short, heavy set, and all gray. And me, I was just little. But I must admit, we did look exceptionally nice in our dressy outfits.

A serpentine garden hose laid coiled at Mr. Walter's feet, spitting a steady stream of water down the driveway. The stream continued its procession into the street and slithered curbside, as we descended down the hill. I was humming some sort of nursery rhyme to myself, the way that little girls often do when they are happy and in their own little sheltered world. I believe it was "Itsy Bitsy Spider". It was a pretty day with the exception of a few dark clouds that seemed to loom in the shadows. I didn't think much of the stealthy stream that accompanied us, that is, until we got to the top of the hill.

"Mama, I think the water is following us."

"Christy, we don't have time for your imaginative stories right now, sweetie. We are just barely going to make it to mass." Mama grabbed my hand and pulled me along as I looked over my shoulder, mesmerized by just how steep the hill was we had just climbed.

"Mama, how did the water . . . ?"

"C'mon, Christy. Stop dragging your feet, baby. No time for sightseeing."

Before I knew it, the road had ended. We had reached the long awaited grassy hill. It was a monstrous expanse of rolling reeds, soft lavender perennials, and vibrant dandelions that took a good five minutes to descend. I was always the first one down, pretending to fly, like a gull scouring the fields of barley below. When we finally reached the bottom, everyone was there, made up real pretty in their floral gowns and hats. The flowers proceeded to seat themselves in the pews, as the wind from the rolling reeds drew a heavy breath, and nudged the lumbering wooden doors closed with a disapproving groan.

13

5

A Tempest with Intention
(S.S. Sentinel - Coast of Costa Rica)

"Top a the mornin', lieutenant."

"A lovely mornin' indeed, captain"

"A little choppy today . . . kind of unusual under the circumstances, wouldn't you say, lieutenant?"

"Sir?"

"No nautical gale lieutenant, not even a breath. And the gulls . . . I haven't seen a one out here in weeks."

"Was thinking the very same thing, sir. Couldn't quite put my finger on it, but now that you mention it . . . no wind, no gulls, kinda strange, sir." The two men stared out into the abyss of ocean, surveying the distant storm clouds on the horizon.

"Captain, is it just me or did this crazy current just shift? It was flowing due west thirty seconds ago. Unless Bernie put some a them special mushrooms in the pesto sauce last night, that current is headed east!" The captain stroked the white of his beard, his weathered blue eyes scoured the churning sea as it nipped rabidly at the hull of the valiant vessel.

"Kinda like the gods are angry, huh? Perhaps the romance between the moon and tide is on the rocks. Eh, captain?"

The captain stared incessantly at the horizon, completely dismissing the lieutenant's poetic allegation. "Honestly, lieutenant ... I'm more concerned with those clouds. I've never seen the likes of them. Them clouds have intention!"

6

A Paradigm Shift

Mr. Lipman shifted the bridge of his thick framed bifocals, wiped the sweat from his brow, and paused for what seemed like an eternity, "The Bible . . . our Holy Bible, the tenets we have held sacred all these years, the very truth to our existence . . . it . . . it . . ."

"What is it, sir?" the general implored delicately.

"It . . . it is . . . to put it bluntly, gentleman . . . I'm afraid it's nothing more than rubbish! Fictitious rubbish!" The room went silent. Mr. Lipman lifted the glasses from his nose, removed the handkerchief from his breast pocket, and wiped a trickling bead of sweat from his furrowed brow.

"What are you saying, sir?"

"The text these boys have found, it seems, is one hundred percent authentic! It speaks of The Holy Bible as a means to keep humanity in line: an obedience instruction manual, if you will."

The visibly shaken scholar paused for a brief moment, and thumbed nervously through the dusty pages, "Dear God, I need to examine this thoroughly."

Mr. Lipman gathered his composure, and with a slight well in his voice, implored, "Dear sirs, please excuse me for I need a moment to myself." The book lay on the black pillow, as the overhead fluorescent exposed a concentric myriad of disheveled stares and jaws wide open. Mr. Lipman hobbled back from the lavatory, his face drenched with a baptism of consolatory tap water.

"How do we know this is not a hoax?" the general asked respectfully.

"Gentlemen, these pages you see before you were printed on ancient Egyptian papyrus, and have miraculously survived thousands and thousands of years underneath the barren sands. It seems a sort of mucus like preservative, the likes of which I have never seen, has aided in its unlikely, yet remarkable perpetuity. The curious structure of the vellum and parchment spine are of equal significance."

The general paused for a moment, "Perpetuity of vellum and who?"

"You must trust me on this, my good men! General, I will need to examine this immediately. Please, if you would be so kind as to let me get back to work.

"Of course, Mr. Lipman. Please let us know if there is anything else you need."

Mr. Lipman slowly slid his glasses down the bridge of his nose, and looked the general square in the eyes with grave concern, "I *will* need one thing from you."

"Sir?" the general inquired, as the other men left the room.

"I beg of you, dear sir, we must keep the information at hand to ourselves, under all circumstances! We must not leak any of this until more conclusive examinations have been exhausted; the consequences would surely be devastating."

"Very well, sir," the general conceded. "Do you really believe this to be true?"

Mr. Lipman rose to his feet, hobbled around the perimeter of the oval table, and planted his feet close enough to slow dance with the general, "I fear, my good sir, that life as we know it has just changed forever."

7

This Just In

Even before the news broke, the change had already begun to occur. As Mr. Lipman worked painstakingly through the night, the signs were insidiously presenting themselves. Clusters of townsfolk stood gathered in the squares watching the morning news,

> *This just in . . . inexplicable cloud cover shrouds most of the northern and southern hemispheres. Most, if not all of the city's zoos have reported their animals to have stopped eating. Many have succumb to unexplained stress and are on the verge of starvation and death. Fisherman harvesting the Panama Gulf, the Red Sea, and the California Coast have reported pockets of dead and rotting fish floating on the surface. Wes Adams, who runs Wes's Bait and Tackle in Seaside, said yesterday, "I ain't seen nothing like it in the twenty years I been here. You got a buffet of rotting fish drifting down wind, and not a single gull to be found. Not a single one.*

8

A Most Curious Sermon

I was only seven, but I remember it like it was yesterday. It was a hot June morning. The townsfolk were all about, watching the TV sets in the window of Harley's Appliance Store. The wind seemed to carry the discourse through the square, beyond the absence of birds atop the big ol' oak, underneath which Mrs. Skully always chained Moses, her beloved black lab. I could see it all, just outside the beautiful stained glass window by our seat. We probably wouldn't have heard it if the birds were there like they usually were, but we did, despite Mrs. Skully's dog carrying on, barking up a storm. Mama looked like she was at her wit's end - between me whining about how hungry I was and asking a million questions, the noise from the square, the incessant barking, and those damn flickering lights that no one else seemed to notice, it was no wonder.

Mama was a devout Christian, born and raised in Southern Oklahoma. Grew up in the Bible Belt and Tornado Alley. Grew up with the fear of Jesus, and twisters, I reckon. Come to think of it, our house was pretty damn near bein' a church: Jesus in every room, a Bible in every drawer, and excerpts of *The Book of This* and *The Book of That* over every aperture.

As I fidgeted on the unforgiving wooden pew, I remember seeing a shadow momentarily stain the sun, as if a plane or something had flown over. Whatever it was, I couldn't hear it over the escalating discourse outside the church. Just then, Moses yelped, and a burst of rain pelted the stained glass window. I was closest and didn't think

18

anyone else heard it. I nonchalantly looked around as Pastor Connelly, with his bald head and black chasuble, preached a poignant verse from the *Book of Isaiah,* *"Even so their roots shall become rotten and their blossom scatter like dust."* It was indeed a solemn sentiment. Little did I know the implication it would have in the coming moments. Honestly, the only thing I was thinking was, "When are we going to eat, and why can't they put a half an inch of padding on these godforsaken seats!?"

9

Revelation

By now Mr. Lipman had confirmed his darkest fears. The single most important text known to mankind had been refuted. The sacred writings that had shed light on, and accounted for, our very existence for thousands and thousands of years had been discounted, and reduced to a shallow puddle of fiction. But something far more terrifying had been unveiled; the Lord that had created the heavens and the earth, the sun and the moon, and all of mankind, had been replaced by a sinister force, the likes of which seemed to elude temporal translation.

"I'm afraid, Gentlemen, that I have some dreadful news. It seems this species or whatever it is we have exhumed, has only bad intentions. Unless the words are only meant to be of threat, I suggest we take appropriate measures and precautions."

"Who in God's name wrote this rubbish!?" the general inquired defensively.

"*What* in God's name, is the question, my good sir. As for the elusive author, I'm afraid the only discernible descriptions we have to go on are along the lines of *amorphous* and *ubiquitous*, neither of which sound very promising."

"Sounds like your typical god-like qualities to me, sir," a young soldier interjected.

"Perhaps, my good man, perhaps indeed. But according to this, a loving and forgiving god it is not! It seems by unearthing this godforsaken tome, we have broken some sort of covenant, and set the wheels of something cataclysmic into motion. See for yourselves, gentlemen." The disheveled old man moved the menacing transcription into the dim light of his dwindling candle,

Liber Exitium - The Book of Doom

Thou conceived from seeds of tedium

Shall infest the ground and flourish

Thereafter, thou shall be granted a book of verses to obey

Behold, the tiller of the soil, should he unearth the pages

Shall reap no more

All life shall cease, big and small

Whirls shall be set upon the plains

And the waters shall become foul and sickly

10

God Rest Ye Naval Gentlemen

The ominous encroaching nimbus clouds infiltrated the Sentinel like a fleet of fighter jets in a matter of seconds, eclipsing the midday sun completely. The solitary ship was suddenly blanketed in darkness; the vast ocean its only witness. The frenzied currents pounded the hull like famished wolves, spinning the mammoth vessel on its central axis. The steel hull creaked and groaned as the twelve hundred meter ship changed direction like a compass needle.

"Mayday! Mayday! I repeat! This is Captain Callahan of the *U.S.S. Sentinel*. We are experiencing some sort of bizarre, inexplicable weather pattern . . . our coordinates are as follows . . ."

A deafening bolt of blue emanated from the depths of the pernicious plumes, exploding the control room from the inside out. A churning ball of fire rolled into the virtual night sky as Captain Callahan and four other decorated crewmen were instantaneously charred, dismembered, and thrown into the awaiting frenzied sea. Despite the unearthly thrust of electrons, not a single clap of thunder was heard. The angry sea stifled, and suddenly settled like a pristine northern lake, bestilling the ensnared vessel in an eerie calm. The remaining crew rushed to the rails, mesmerized by the glass like state of the deep blue.

"I . . . I think it's over!" a nervous deckhand stuttered.

"You might wanna rethink that, swabbie," another stern faced sailor cracked, as he lit up a smoke and gestured towards the hull.

The glassy sea began to arc surreally, slowly pulling the ship into a concentric encapsulating concavity. The hull groaned as her weight flexed the monstrous vessel upon itself.

"What the fuck is happening!!?"

"Damned if I know, swabbie! It ain't no whirlpool! It ain't even spinnin'!"

The hull creaked for the last time. A convex vertical wave pummeled through the center of the lanky steel frame, lifted the forty-five thousand ton battleship out of the water, and ripped it in half like a WWII depth charger. The enormous ship disappeared beneath the surface, pulling everything in its vicinity underneath the dark sea. The wind whispered, and the colossal ship was gone, as if she had never existed. The deafening silence mustered a gentle breeze, as the sinister sky repented, and relinquished its reign. The clouds scattered, and the violated sun reluctantly breathed a shameful breath upon the endless sea, as if nothing had ever happened. The history books will chalk it up to inexplicable magnetic fields or enormous methane bubbles from the dark depths of the ocean, but the eighteen hundred brave crewman of the *U.S.S. Sentinel* shall remain the select few to bear witness to the unlikely events of that fateful day, and shall forever take their secrets to their watery graves.

11

Darkness

I remember praying for mass to be over because my stomach was rumbling like the encroaching storm clouds, just outside the beautiful stained glass window to my left.

"Can we go now? I'm hungry! I'm bored! When are we leaving!?" I whined relentlessly. "Christy, be quiet! I'm not gonna say it again! We are in church!" Mama screamed under her breath. Jeffrey, Mrs. Wilderbee's boy, was playing cars next to me with another boy. I started teasing them while they played with their cherished little hot wheels collection.

"God, why do boys love those things?!"

"Christy, leave those boys alone," Mama yelled. "They are minding their own business."

"Mommy's little angels," I thought to myself. "I bet their mamas never make them starve!" Well, I went right back to teasing. Looking back now, if I was Mama, I would've slapped some sense into me. I knocked the 57 Pontiac straight off the pew. It landed wheels down, *Smokey and the Bandit* style, and proceeded to roll straight towards Pastor Connelly. That's when Mama lost it! Between the ranting outside in the square, a hysterical canine, and the intermittent flickering light show, that by now, had infected each station of the cross, it was all she could bear. Mama stood up, her cheeks crimson with embarrassment, and grabbed my arm with a jolt, "That's it, young lady! We are going home! Right now!!! Mama clenched my wrist like a lunatic! Little Jeffrey was wailing like it was the end of the world . . . little did he know. Suddenly, her hand loosened around my wrist and dropped lifelessly to her side, as she realized the whole congregation was fixated on the front door. It was Mrs. Wilkinson.

My memories of Mrs. Wilkinson were always fond. She was a jovial soul, perpetually pinching my cheeks, ever so annoyingly. Seeing her like that, I was so scared. She was just standing there, drenched, her hair pelted flat. I only knew her as the woman with the two-story beehive - a dignified woman, composed in beautiful floral dresses, adorned with flawlessly matching accessories. She stood there with her neck leaning completely to one side like she had lost all muscle control. She gazed at the rafters above the altar, as the rain slammed the roof of the silent church. That's what I remember. She just stood there like that for what seemed like a lifetime. I was terrified. No one said anything. There was just the rain. Suddenly her eyes shifted towards the giant crucifix over Pastor Connelly's head, "You are all praying in vain!!!" she screeched in a horrible gargled burst. Her knees buckled, and her head hit the floor with a sickening muffled thud.

As the blood flowed down the aisle, memories of flower girls and beautiful white dresses disappeared, forever replaced by the sight of Mrs. Wilkinson's limp, lifeless body. The flickering lights blew out with a pop as Mama pulled me into her sheltering embrace. Her warm hands covered my frozen eyes, but it was too late. The darkness was upon me.

12

We Interrupt This Program . . .

As the ocean caressed the pristine Costa Rican coastline just outside their window, Arman and Sansar were learning of the news for the first time. Every single channel spewed the word of the maniacal new gospel, just as Mr. Lipman had feared, and all corners of the globe were now privy to the unnerving revelations, and the reality of a potential extermination.

. . . *Suicide rates reach alarming highs worldwide. Criminal activity continues to go unprecedented. Jumpers in Manhattan, suicide pacts in Paris, Looting in Louisiana, prescription pills in Peking. Bodies smolder, littering rails across the English countryside. People wander streets aimlessly: confused, despondent, displaced. It seems most of the work force has simply surrendered. The economy continues to crumble as stocks plummet to the red. Recession is imminent. Anarchy is upon us. I am afraid to say, this just may be . . . (static consumes the broadcast)*

"Holy shit! Are you seeing this, Sansar? What the hell did we find out there?"

"I told you we had something, little brother. I told you, did I not?"

"It's nice to see someone was lucid enough to adorn their captioning with a bit of clever alliteration as people are offing themselves," Sansar joked, not yet realizing the severity of the situation. Arman quickly dismissed his brother's shallow contribution to the conversation, and stared into the flickering

26

screen. Suddenly the interference ceased, and the caption on the screen was as clear as day,

. . . God is dead! We are now at war with God knows what! All we can do now is wait!

"This is madness!" Arman uttered, as his jaw hit the floor. The static abstained long enough for the brothers to learn the whole truth, and all of its gory details, before the screen went black for the last time.

"Strangely, my brother, I am not shocked. I mean, yes, the whole hostile creature thing taking over the planet, well yeah, that's a little shocking. But the invalidation of our so called Good Book? That was inevitable," Sansar boasted with an "I told you so grin". I mean, I always knew it, somewhere deep in my heart, but I guess there's always that glimmer of hope. But that's all it is, or was . . . "hope". People like to call it faith, but what's the fucking difference? It ain't nothin' but another word for hope. We believe what we wanna believe, my friend. We wanna believe it so bad that we've tricked ourselves into believing it all these years."

Sansar glanced out at the intensifying whitecaps as they pounded the sand like distant drummers, "You remember that time Mama told us about the girl who was trapped in that well for seven days? I remember Mama saying that girl prayed her ass off for six nights straight, and said she never felt so alone. She said she knew right then that there was no God. On the seventh day she cut off her limb. What does that say, man?" Sansar looked up at the photo of their beloved mother above the mantelpiece and shook his head in disgust, still bitter from her untimely passing.

"I remember being in some little place down in Williamsburg, before Mama got sick. You were just a kid at the time. There was this girl playing, you know with an acoustic guitar, and she did this song she wrote about this void in her life, this big hole, and how much she wanted to fill that space. She sang this song, it was like she was pleading with God to show himself, or at the very least give her a sign. She was crying while she was singing it, man! I'll never forget that." The two brothers sat silently in the dim light as the static illuminated the room with an eerie glow. Arman watched a tear roll from his brother's cheek, as his tall, lanky silhouette gazed into the abyss of the flickering fluorescent,

"What's next? Wait, let me guess . . . *Christians despondent, atheists profess their litanies of 'I told you so's', and agnostics don't know what the fuck to think. Tune in at eleven for complete coverage.*"

"Ha ha," Arman replied sarcastically, warranting an evil grimace from his cynical sibling, "And I do remember Mama's story. But there simply must be a God! We are so complex. I mean, we are made up of billions of cells. Our bodies heal themselves. Women conceive and give birth. Do you realize how amazing that is!? We can see, hear, and feel. We feel love! Real love! Love so strong that it must transcend death, it simply must!"

Sansar, still transfixed on the eerie static filled screen responded apathetically, as if he were bathing in the same pool of sorrows as the rest of the nation, "You say this because you want it so badly, my brother. We all do. This is why this book has been our lifeblood. It has given us hope. It has given us heaven! A reward and reason for our measly fucking existence, and a contract to ensure we will see our loved ones when we die. Well, so much for that shit. We got nothin' now. For thousands of years we believed in this book! We may as well believe in John fucking Edwards or the fucking Loch Ness Monster. Maybe all this talk about aliens and pyramids is not that far fetched after all. Oh Look! I think I just saw Bigfoot rollerblading down the boardwalk!"

"Why can't you ever be serious?" Arman huffed.

"I *am* serious! Look . . . he's the one pulling the Seven Dwarfs and the Tooth Fairy on his sleigh."

13

There's Something in the Water

With each flip of a page, the ominous text professed its intention. The smell of fear and despair wafted through the city's streets as the summer's biggest page turner reared its ugly head. With a lump in his throat and torment on his tongue, Mr. Lipman, the mentally exhausted lingual prodigy proceeded to read on,

The very element that sustained thee for a thousand years

Shall be relinquished

And thee shall stand no higher than a pile of dust

As mighty oaks fall, become barren and perish

So shall thee become barren and perish

As great lakes and rivers turn to dust

So shall thee be turned to dust

As oceans and seas shrivel and become dry and lifeless

So shall thee become dry and lifeless.

In a futile attempt to regain his composure, the distraught Englishman dipped his finger into the glass of ice water sitting at the edge of his dimly lit desk, and flicked the contents onto his sweaty brow. The drops infiltrated his pours as if his face a virgin sponge.

The visibly shaken scholar, too distraught to realize the oddity of the infiltration, cleared his throat and resumed his interpretation of the dark pages,

> *For ye not swept away by whirls and left to perish on plains*
>
> *Shall be dragged to sea by salty towers that touch the sky*
>
> *Those that remain*
>
> *Like scattered insects infesting the soil*
>
> *Shall be reduced to no more than pillars of salt*

14

Itsy Bitsy Spider

Outside, I could see the wind picking up, but dare not say a word. I can remember standing in the corner of the church, but don't quite recall how I ended up there. I must have backed up as everyone ran to Mrs. Wilkinson. Mama was too busy trying to wipe the blood from her face to even notice. It was like everyone in the church was in a frenzy, scurrying and scuffling about, and I just stood there in my own reverie, watching, like a director of some gothic tragedy. It was almost as if I had a sixth sense of some sort. Everything I didn't want to see was in slow motion, but everything else transpired in real time.

I could hear the rain slam the stained glass furiously as the wind howled at our holy little haven. It was what I didn't hear that drew me toward the window. The barking had stopped. I assumed Moses had just given up, succumb to the storm. As I reluctantly inched my way toward the few sections of glass that were clear enough to reveal the ruckus, or lack thereof, I saw Moses at the foot of the old oak. He was completely sprawled out, like a compass, each limb pointing in a different direction. I remember it was hard to focus as the rain flushed the smoky glass. I couldn't be sure if what I saw was just the imagination of a seven-year old little girl or something much worse. Moses looked like a giant black spider sitting at the foot of the swaying tree, almost as though he was flattened out by something. A horrible, drenched, flattened giant black spider.

The lights were still flickering, only worse now. My face felt cool on the glass. Looking back, I must have been in shock because I just stood there staring at the swaying tree, the very tree that gave me comfort on Sunday mornings past. It rocked back and forth over the spider that was once Moses. I heard Pastor Connelly yell to one of the alter boys to tend the back door that flew open from the howling winds. Amidst the escalating commotion, I noticed something about the tree. It had stopped swaying. The wind was as strong as before, but the tree was still.

It was then that I saw it change. I should've been scared but could not look away. The roots seemed to shrivel and burrow back into the earth. The bark from the base of the tree peeled and turned black. The corrosion ascended toward the branches like an infectious mold slithering from the ground. The lower branches snapped first. As the insidious blight reached the summit, a large limb fell onto the spider that lay at the foot of the dying oak. Moses scattered like ashes into the darkening landscape. As the blackness consumed the mammoth oak, the leaves withered, and rained down like black ash before my eyes. The base wobbled and the goliath oak leaned in for the kill.

"Mama!!!" I screamed. Before I could even get the words out, the trunk breached the upper rafters.

"Christy!!! Christy!!!" Mama cried. She grabbed my hand so tight I saw stars. I also saw the gaping wounds on her wrists as she whisked me underneath the Virgin Mary overlooking the rows of votive candles. Oddly enough, every single one of the candles remained burning.

15

Central Weather Bureau - Taipei City, Taiwan

Moisture rising from the Gulf, clashing with cool air from the Rockies, has spawned a violent rampage of severe weather throughout the Midwest. News crews frantically attempt to capture footage in hopes of alerting the public before all communication is lost.

Rich Nesman - *CWB: We go to Les Hardy, who is covering the outbreak of twisters in Des Moines. There is speculation these storms are forming from abnormal oceanic activity. Is there any truth to this speculation? If so, can you shed some light on this most bizarre weather pattern?*

Les Hardy - *KCCI News 8: Rich, these conditions are completely correlated with oceanic activity. The weather, quite simply, is contingent upon the water cycle. The weather is practically run by it. You name it, Rich - tornadoes, hurricanes, thunderstorms, blizzards, rain - they are all related to this capricious and sometimes volatile cycle. As we know, tornadoes form when wet, hot air meets dry, cool air. Hurricanes form from differences in air and water temperature. Thunderstorms are made of clouds, and blizzards are just frozen water. But this? This system seems to disavow everything we have learned. Historically, this kind of weather system is unprecedented. We have never seen this kind of activity. Never! The sheer volume, ferocity, and behavior, quite frankly, is beyond me. This is, by far, the most prolific storm pattern I, for one, have ever seen in my career. My God, this is unbelievable! There are . . .*

Rich Nesman: *Les, are you still with us? Les . . . Les . . . It sounds like we've lost audio. I can't believe the footage I'm seeing. I can only imagine what Les must be dealing with out there. We will be keeping you updated with any information regarding this storm pattern throughout the evening. We will continue to provide a list of shelters throughout the night as the storms intensify. This is Rich Nesman signing off. May God be with you all tonight.*

16

What Things Shall Come

"You said the girl in the well felt nothing, no presence of God, when she chopped off her limb on the seventh day. Do you not think *that* was a miracle? Not everyone has the strength to do *that*. Where did that strength come from? And what were the odds that amongst all those ancient rusted artifacts sitting at the bottom of that well, there was a saw? I don't know, Sansar. To me that is a miracle!" Sansar glanced across the coffee table, as the mumble of morbid news muddied the room, and the gauntlet of flickering lights illuminated the hallway like a funhouse at some strange carnival. He looked adoringly at his little brother, for those were the things he loved most about him—his innocence and trusting naivety.

Sansar spoke softly as a tear rolled down his iron cheek, "Do you remember when we were kids and Father didn't come home that night? I know you were only eleven, but a sixteen- year old boy can see the emptiness in his mother's eyes. I knew she knew that would be the last time we would ever see him. You never saw how scared she was because she hid it from you. She was strong, Mama was, but she told me, years later, how she thought of taking her own life many times. We were the only thing that kept her alive all those years. She busted her ass taking care of us, you know that? She even scraped away enough for your stupid swim lessons. Alot a good they did ya, you still tread water like a drowning rat. Then what? After all that, she ends up with lymphoma and fucking suffers for years!" Sansar wiped his eyes in disgust, "How the fuck can you justify that?"

Arman, too distraught to recount the grim memories, mustered up a saucy grin, "You ain't exactly Michael Phelps, either. Doesn't mean this rat can't beat an old fool like you".

The brother's laughter, as unenthusiastic as it may have been, cut the tension like a knife, like a desert rose pleading for an imminent flood.

"We'll see about that," Sansar uttered facetiously. "We'll see about that."

17

S.S. Ariel - Southeast of Easter Island

"Holy shit! You feel that, Admiral!?"

"Did I feel that?!! It felt like a blue whale just swam underneath the hull!" Admiral Brady immediately got on the horn to NOAA (National Oceanic and Atmospheric Administration) aka (NO-ah)

"Tell me you guys didn't get a reading on that! That was no run of the mill rogue wave!"

NOAA, Kauai, Hawaii: "Sir, we've been getting reports of activity like this all over: The Western Atlantic, The Gulf of Mexico, The Indian Ocean, you name it. Funny thing is, there's no seismic activity to be found. Honestly sir, I am beside myself. All I know is whatever it was must have originated within a very small radius of your coordinates because there is no record of this thing on our radar."

Brady removed his cap and scoured the horizon, which now presented an eerie calm, "With all due respect, sir, whatever it was, it's headed directly towards the Costa Rican coastline, and 4.5 million people, at a furious rate. We need to get everyone off that coast now!!"

The sirens screamed through the streets like the clanging chimes of doom. The locals, including Arman and Sansar, were no strangers to the sound, for they had heard it many times before. Countless drills and warnings had prepared them for the inevitable. But could it prepare them for the unthinkable?

18

A Mother's Love

Mama could see the fear in my eyes as the wind blew clouds of black ash and rain into the church's open wound. There was so much noise, so much screaming. She grabbed my face in her hands and held me tightly so I could see nothing except for her loving eyes. Mama made all the screams go away.

"Christy, do you remember when you were a little girl? You are such a big girl now, but you were so beautiful . . . and so smart. You were lying on the couch, deep in thought, and you asked Grandma, you said, 'Grandma, why are we here?' Do you remember that, baby?" I nodded reluctantly as my tears slowly began to abate.

"She said, 'God made us, sweetie. He made you . . . me . . . Mommy . . . he made everyone.' Then you said, 'If God made us, then who made God?' And Grandma said, 'No one made God, sweetie. God was always here.' Mama gently held my face and brushed my tears with her thumbs.

"Do you remember that, baby? Do you remember how upset you were? How that just didn't sit right with you? It never made sense to you, baby, I know. Then Hailey was born . . . and you said, 'I think I believe in God now, Mommy.' And you smiled . . . you smiled just like you're smiling now . . . that beautiful little smile."

19

Apocalypsis Iesu Christi

As the moonlight glazed the glistening London streets, Mr. Lipman toiled away, struggling to decipher the ancient pages that likely preceded our Holy Bible by thousands of years. As he fervently scurried through the scripts, his hands shook, fearing each foreboding paragraph. The book itself was daunting. Its black and rotted cover reeked of unholiness, yet the stature and girth of the text were that of three bibles. It laid six inches deep and its face the size of a checkerboard. There were symbols etched into the giant black cover, many of which resembled that of archaic fish drawn by an imaginative five year old. The kind of crude etchings one might find in a desolate cave or remote archeological dig. The writings were etched in lengthy verses, each more grave than the next, and spoke of "creatures that have always been among us." Mr. Lipman requested solitude as he descended into the dark pages, for he knew he had only scratched the surface.

As the dead of night crawled into London Town, the weary Englishman's eyes grew heavy under the dimming candlelight that softly illuminated the old Victorian armchair he now called home. As he dozed off, the ratio of chin sweat and cranium weight forced his head to slip from his propped elbow with a jolt. Startled by his own convulsion, he awoke to a ray of light, a ray of moonlight that seemed to highlight a verse adjacent to the black tasseled bookmark he laid on the page, anticipating the morning light. Like a burning bush, *Revelatio* reflected in the lenses of his old tattered bifocals. The correlation was immediately apparent,

"The last book of the New Testament, *The Book of Revelation* - in which St. John wrote *Apocalypsis Iesu Christi*. Of course! Of course it's a revelation! A revelation of what?" Mr. Lipman mumbled aloud. "No sleep for the weary," he sighed. "At least not tonight." Every subsequent chapter thus far had warned of impending doom and the evils to come, yet somehow he knew that this time, it was going to be far worse.

> *Behold, the Lord sayeth unto thee*
>
> *Ye that roam thy barren plain like cattle*
>
> *Shall feareth thy pages and abide thy verses*
>
> *Thy God thou shalt not see*
>
> *Thou shalt not hear*
>
> *Thou shalt not feel*
>
> *As it shall be granted in the Book of Old*
>
> *'Ye shall take the shield of faith,*
>
> *Wherewith ye shall quench the fiery darts of the wicked*
>
> *Trust in the Lord with all thine heart; and lean not unto thine own understanding'*
>
> *Thou shall abide like ants*
>
> *Fearing the weight of a hundred soles*
>
> *If one hundred shall stray*
>
> *One hundred shall perish*
>
> *Wind, rain, and famine shall cleanse the plains*
>
> *Water shall flow red, like wine*
>
> *Red like the blood of hanged cattle*
>
> *Back into the sea*

20

A Prayer for the Dying

I wondered how all those candles continued to burn, despite the lashes of wind and rain. A cloud of black ash eclipsed the statue of Jesus that hung helplessly above the altar, overlooking the ensuing chaos. Mrs. Raphael was tending Mama's wound when I noticed that a single votive candle had blown out. Suddenly, the parish doors blew open like a cannon! It was Mrs. Hubble, from the Jumble Hobby Shop; a reclusive old woman who lived above the store and spent much of her time with her two black cats. She stumbled down the isle, drenched and smothered in soot, oblivious to the wreckage. "You are all going to die!" she screamed, as the water rolled off her brimstone hat and ran down the aisle that, once upon a time, bore such sweet memories. "People are being swept away! Swept away by the whirls! At least that's what they're calling them on the news!" the woman uttered in a frantic Southern drawl. "They're hittin' Missouri, Wichita, Iowa, Dallas, you name it! The finger of God is upon us! And waves . . . waves as high as mountains are swallowing up the coast! God help us all! You all need to leave this church before it's too late!"

Mama grabbed my hand and pulled me into her arms once again. This time it was my ears she covered. She tried to muffle the words, but I could still see the fear in poor old Mrs. Hubble's eyes. She didn't have to say a single word, her eyes said it all. I knew . . . even at seven years old . . . I knew.

21

The Monster in the Mirror

It was Sunday morning, the midday sun reflected off the playful whitecaps that rolled gently onto the shore. The beach was a stone's throw from the deck of Sansar and Arman's humble seaside apartment. The pristine sands that were normally saturated with tourists and locals alike were abandoned. The lonely granules swirled concentrically across the vast landscape of the tropical ghost town. A balmy breeze crept underneath the blinds of the large patio window that faced the ocean by the kitchen table, from which the view was absolutely breathtaking. On the far side of the apartment was Arman's computer, which faced the back wall. On a clear day, in power-saver mode, one could see the ocean's reflection so clearly you'd think you were peering out the window. Arman had just attempted to send an email to their sister Nousha in Dubai. The networks were overloaded with frantic transmissions. Outside discourse had been next to impossible. Sansar, disgusted with the lack of reception, reached blindly into the depths of the refrigerator, like Indiana Jones finagling his hand through a gauntlet of exotic arthropods and insects, and fumbled for the elusive Banana Snapple - the holy grail of soft drinks.

"C'mon, you little bastard," he muttered, as his fingers grasped the familiar shape of its prized neck. Just then, a glimmer from Arman's idle iMac took him by surprise. A single white strip glistened across the idle screen. "Hey, Arman!" Sansar shouted. "I think the tubes inside your monitor are shot." Sansar moseyed over to the patio window and plopped himself down on the old straw kitchen chair. They both gazed curiously into the screen. A distant rumbling accompanied the faint thickening line. The hairs on the back of their necks began to stand on edge as they put two and two together, and realized that the white fluctuating line they were witnessing was not internal, but a reflection of the distant horizon. The two brothers slowly turned in complete unison, and in a perfect synchronous gasp, produced the same exact sentiment, "Holy Shit!" The sirens screamed through the streets the second the words escaped their lips. The white line roared a hundred miles off shore and stretched as far as the eye could see, slithering across the horizon, smirking from ear to ear.

Sansar grabbed his little brother by the cheek, "Arman, look at me. Do you remember what we planned the last time the sirens went off? Do you remember?" he inquired in a calm collected voice.

Arman shook uncontrollably as his eyes began to well, "We rrrun down Seaside Boulevard until wwe hit higher ground?"

"That's right," Sansar said sternly, exhibiting no fear, doing his best to comfort him. "We don't stop running until we reach higher ground, and we don't turn around. Got it?"

Arman brushed his eyes and kissed his brothers face, "I love you, my broth . . . "

Sansar put his hand over Arman's mouth, "No time for mush now, just remember what I said, 'Don't Look Back'. Now run! . . . RUN!!!!" Arman stumbled over every possible inanimate object before finding his way to the hallway. Sansar blasted through the door first, surprised to see the others in the building lingering with a minimal sense of urgency.

"Is it real this time? Surely it's not," a voice chimed out from a cluster of tenants congregating in the stairwell.

"Look for yourselves!" Sansar insisted, as he pointed towards the horizon and forced his way through the herd.

The distant thin line was now a thick burst of white fury, roaring in the distance. As the two brothers emptied out of the stairwell and onto the boulevard, the distant rumble emptied Arman's bladder with no apologies. As the urine ran down his leg, the familiar burn triggered an old locked away childhood memory . . .

I'd only peed myself once before in my entire life. We were leaving the old boat yard down by the marina, a half-mile from my house. I was thirteen years old. I hopped the fence first, my pumas nervously rattled the giant "No Trespassing" sign hung from the rungs. The fence was high, maybe ten feet. I hit the ground first. My "buddies", Kumar and Lazarus hesitated. At that very moment, a squad car streaked by the gauntlet of retired fishing boats, dousing any hopes of freedom. Logically, I ran away from the black and white, and towards the beckoning gates of salvation. There was no St. Peter there to greet me. Instead, I ran face first into the waiting arms of a black uniform flaunting a shiny gold badge. He threw me against that squad car like I was a twenty-one year old felon. His partner appeared magically and joined the interrogation,

"Where are your friends!? What are their names!?

I clammed up like a barnacle on the hull of one those damn boats, "They're just some kids I met," I answered, sheepishly.

"I think we should take him down to the station. What do ya think, Gus? And any damage to these boats, kid, whether you did it or not, you are going to pay for it!" Well, I evacuated right then and there; a warm burst of joy ran down my leg, completely saturating my crotch. I wasn't sure if they noticed, but they let me go just about then, so I'm thinking they did. They just wanted to scare the shit out of me. Lucky that didn't happen! And there I was, walking home with my tail between my legs, and a big puddle in my pants, when . . .

"ARMAN!!! FOR GOD'S SAKE!!! SNAP OUT OF IT!! MOVE YOUR DAMN FEET!!!"

. . . and just like that I was back. I now understand why some folks devise split personalities to deal with unbearable fear or pain! Disoriented by my regressive stroll down memory lane, I defied my brother's one and only request, and looked back at the sea. It was no longer a distant crest. I could see the white water churning. Somehow it didn't behave like the monster waves I'd seen on TV. It seemed to somehow disobey the very principles of earthly physics. I could see the rows of water roll off of one another, like a pack of starved wolves clawing over each other to get at the kill. Just as my skin began to crawl, I felt something latch onto my wrist like a vice, "What the fuck did I tell you!?" Sansar screamed. "We are not going to die here, now run before I kill you myself!" I clumsily resumed stride.

I could no longer hear the screams from the beach, which by now, was a good half-mile behind us. Suddenly, a burst of wind seemed to come out of nowhere, almost knocking me to the pavement. I felt a sharp spray of cold water whip the back of my neck, and just like that it was gone. The faint scream of sirens was suddenly trifled by a sickly compressed roar that reverberated in my chest. It was then that I realized why the screams from the beach had ceased. My heart sank, as I said a prayer for those we left behind: the elderly, the disabled, the children! I could only imagine what they had witnessed. I remained faithful to my brother's wish, and didn't look back, not even for a moment. Sansar was a few body lengths ahead, but I could see him glance peripherally, every few seconds, to track my position. My lungs were screaming for air and my will was quickly fading.

Up ahead lay a huge glass mirrored building, at least twenty-stories high. "Higher ground is just beyond this building!!!" Sansar yelled, as he gasped for air. With every successive step, the monster in the mirror presented itself in the giant mirrored panels. Its presence could now be seen, heard, and felt, in pristine fidelity. Exhausted and hopeless, the two brothers collapsed at the foot of the building, staring up at the goliath panes of mirror that captured the encroaching beast like an IMAX theatre. Three black juxtaposed sixes glistened at the top of the building, exclaiming their final destination, "That figures?" Sansar sighed, as he surrendered his last breath. The sea rose, like a wall of water. It moved furiously, as if it were rising straight up toward the sky. The last thing I felt was the weight of Sansar's lanky frame attempting to shelter me from the end of the world, "Make Mama proud, my little brother. Show her those swim lessons weren't a waste of money. I love you, and always will."

22

Fright Night

The lavender lilies adorned the old dusty trail that snaked through town and slithered by the front stoop of the widow Evan's modest rustic cabin, just beyond the old church. Doris still goes by Mrs. Evans, despite losing her husband to a malignant brain tumor three years ago. She swears she still sees his ghost walk the halls every now and again, but his memory haunts her every single day.

Doris was busy scrubbing the dirty dishes she neglected from the morning's dismal breakfast. Disgusted with the lack of reception and flickering lights, she hung her dish towel on the eye hook over the sink, and embarked upon her evening shower. "At least we still have hot water," she thought to herself, as she ran her hand through a plume of steam contained within the panes of misty glass.

Doris Evans had been by herself for the last three years, and was considered the catch of the town to any worthy or fortunate suitor. Doris was the quintessential, petite, blonde, blue-eyed girl-next-door type. She ate well and did her daily runs through the woods by the old psych center, which hadn't seen the light of day since 1949.

Legend has it, that during a particular rainy afternoon run, moments before dusk, she witnessed something that would haunt her for days to come. Doris would often throw on her headphones and get lost in song as she paced her way through the lonely winding trails. As she descended down a particular ravine, she noticed two frail elderly women crossing the path about twenty yards in front of her, one seemed to be helping the other across the trail. They were dressed all in white and moved ever so slowly. As she passed, a terrible uneasiness came over her. Overwhelmed, she turned back to see if they were ok. No more than five seconds had elapsed. She turned to look, and there was nothing. Nothing but the dirge of dusk, crooning to a lonely, painful quietness. She surveyed every possible exit. She knew all too well there was no way, considering the rate of speed and time elapsed, they could have made it out of those trails. Her skin turned cold, as her eyes scoured the darkening woods. Shadows loomed from every branch. Her heart roared, and she ran like she had never run before. To this day, she has never gone back to those trails.

Since the death of her beloved husband, there is little that comforts her. A hot shower and an occasional movie night at home with her best friend, Michele, were the highlights of her depressing existence. Doris possessed an affinity towards the macabre and deemed each Tuesday eve "Fright Night." Like clockwork, Michele would arrive promptly by 9 p.m. and the two would delve bravely into her catalogue of classic horror films.

The night was young, so Doris decided to take advantage, before Michele arrived. As she let her hair down, the steam rolled into her candle lit bedroom, and called out to her like a compelling bedtime page-turner. It crept around the corner, seducing the weary, vulnerable young woman. The steam seemed to take form, as it lured her within the confines of the lavender bathroom walls. She peeled off her petite jean shorts and gently kicked them onto the wet tile floor. She slid her white tank top over her silky shoulders and hung it on the heart shaped hook above the bathroom door. As she peeled her panties, a plume of steam entered her nares, "Oh my . . . too hot . . . even for me," she playfully whispered. She calibrated the shower handle and stepped one leg over the porcelain tub. The water seemed to glimmer over the silkiness of her shapely, tan thigh. As she pulled her other leg in, she exhaled with pleasure, as the hot water consumed her broken soul. The water infiltrated her beautiful straight blonde hair and rolled down her neck, caressing her perfect breasts. She groaned with reckless abandon, "Mmmmm," as she caressed her body with suds of fragrant vanilla. She ran her soapy hands across her buxom chest, down her hips, and over her perfectly heart-shaped cheeks.

Doris always found the heat and steam of her shower to be intensely erotic. As the water trickled down her waist she began to touch herself. She cried softly with pleasure, and writhed against the misty glass, as the hot water drenched her soapy, silken silhouette. She propped her leg upon the edge of the tub and grasped the showerhead, fondling it delicately, as her finger entered her warm waiting lips. Her body tingled with pleasure with every penetrating droplet. As she whimpered in ecstasy, she felt the warm water enter her softly from behind, "Oh God, Oh God, YES! YES!! YES!!!" She threw her head back and pressed her chest against the steamed glass, and came harder than she had in three long years.

The water rained down upon the arch of her back and trickled down her shimmering outstretched ass and trembling thighs. The beads rolled from her bowed head and fell like tears at her feet as she stood quivering and panting with elation, while the imprints of her sweaty palms anointed the steam filled den of iniquity.

As she stood in a state of orgasmic reverie, the sensation of something crawling up her leg forced her eyes open. The hot water that trickled down her leg was now trickling upward. Her elation quickly turned to terror as paralysis consumed her body. The molecules crawled up her thigh like a thousand salacious fingertips, violating her porcelain skin. They proceeded to tighten on her like a vice as they crept up her torso like ivy. She frantically tried to free herself from the confines of the murky stall but her body conceded to the horror. The water itself seemed to take shape as it ascended up her spine. A liquefied rope coiled around her delicate neck forcing her mouth open. The pressure so intense her eyes bulged, yet she could not scream. The hot water rushed down her esophagus, breached her epiglottis, and filled her trachea. She choked and gasped desperately for air. There was no air, only water. She fell to her knees, drowning, slowly and painfully, in the steam filled tomb she once found so comforting. A final desperate gasp for air and she was gone.

The once beautiful creature, and wet dream of every neighborhood boy from here to Dristol County, lay coiled against the dripping glass doors. The steam, content with its lascivious liquidation, evanesced like a wily serpent, and the drops silenced. Michele arrived promptly at 9 p.m. as always, and let herself in. Doris Evans was pronounced dead at approximately 9:15 p.m., Tuesday evening - Fright Night. The autopsy ruled her death - asphyxiation by drowning - yet not a single molecule remained in her lifeless body.

23

The Sufferer's Palace

The choppers and news crews spun their webs of light over the township of Divinity, one of the few stretches of land that remained sacred from the floods. Despite its fidelity to the church, and close proximity to Our Lady, the wholesome town had succumbed to the wicked. Looters and rioters alike, raped the town of her dignity, as the faithful clashed with the faithless. Sam wheeler, the town's handyman, and a devout atheist since his wife Amelia drowned in their tub, was locking horns with Clara Roberts, and a gaggle of church goers, in front of ol' man Greeley's general store. The tale of the tape -Wheeler weighed in at 250 lbs. and stood 6'4". Clara stood about 5' and some change and weighed less than a buck, soaking wet. The bell rang, and Davy and Goliath threw down gloves.

"I refuse to believe it, I refuse! I don't care what they're telling us. God is alive and well!" gasped Mrs. Roberts in a frail, yet forthright voice. "Do you really think this is all coincidence? Is it a coincidence that the sun never fizzles out? That the thermometer never drops so low that we all end up like freeze pops? That it never gets so hot that we all go up like a tinderbox? Is it all just coincidence? And let's not forget about the very element that comprises two-thirds of our big blue marble. The very element we cannot survive without. Do we ever run out of that? Do we ever just die of thirst because we run out of good ol' plentiful H2O? Of course not, because there is a God! A God who love's us!"

Sam Wheeler summoned up the mucus from the back of his throat, and decorated the porch with his vileness. "You God fearing folk got an answer for everything, don't cha? Why'd dat tornado miss dat church and kill everyone else? Because it was God's will. Why'd my boy die, when all the other kids on the school bus lived? It was God's will. Why does the sinner feast while the saint starves? God's will, of course. You people just love to make shit up and tailor it to suit your needs!"

Clara's brow, nestled under the rim of her ruffled Victorian hat, clenched tightly, "You're a bitter man, Mr. Wheeler. You've lost your faith," she professed confidently. "And this is why you are so bitter. You have to feel it in your heart."

Mr. Wheeler laughed facetiously, "Faith? Faith?? Faith is nothing more than a fairytale! Y'all have bowed your heads for thousands of years to the biggest fairytale ever written. Now what cha gonna do? Who ya gonna believe in now? Santa Claus? Jiminy Cricket?"

"I have found God, Mr. Wheeler. And nothing can take that away. You need to search your heart and find the Lord."

"Is that a fact, lady. And just what happened? Did you misplace him? Lose him like an old pair of socks?"

Mrs. Roberts looked at him with pity in her eyes. "Do you have children, Mr. Wheeler? If you did you would know the Lord's love. How could something so beautiful be created by anything other than a loving God?"

Wheeler summoned up an encore of mucus for the front stoop. This time the wind snatched it out of the sky before it had a chance to hit the ground.

"Tell that to all the four-year-old kids in the cancer ward, and their mothers, who get to watch their only child die before they even get a chance to say their first fucking word. That's the God you wanna believe in!? I wouldn't have a kid if you put a gun to my head. For what? To put him through that? Nobody came to me before I was born and said, 'Hey, this is what you can expect . . . you still want in?' There's a fifty-fifty chance you may wake up one morning with a lump in your colon, or blood in your urine, get hooked on drugs, be maimed or horribly burned, or end up suicidal, and a hundred percent chance you will lose both your parents after they raised you and showed you the most love you will ever know. That is, if you were lucky enough not to have been molested, abused or abandoned. Fuck that! Why the hell would I wanna come into a world anything less than Utopian, never mind this fucking mess! This is the sufferer's palace, no place for children! Y'all make me sick."

As he tipped his cap over his empty eyes and began to walk off, a soft timid voice from the midst of the crowd uttered with a pristine innocence, "I'm very sorry about your wife, Mr. Wheeler." Wheeler stopped in his tracks.

"Hush, Jacob, hush!!!" the boy's mother stressed nervously under her breath. Wheeler stood there motionless for what seemed like an eternity. He slowly turned to look at the child. He looked him up and down. His empty eyes shifted towards the boy's mother. She stood motionless, conscious of her own elevated breathing. Wheeler looked back at the child one more time, turned around, and walked away. The congregation waited to exhale as he dragged himself and his bum leg down the middle of the deserted road. The wind rustled through the empty streets as the moon laid its weary head upon its pillow. Darkness descended upon Divinity, and Sam Wheeler faded into her awaiting, unconditional embrace.

24

The Book of Affliction

For a thousand years

And a thousand more

The meek shall be maintained

Saturated with simple solution

Elders shall succumb to attrition

Attrition of critical articulations

Cardiac muscle shall weaken and become necrotic

Infants shall be stillborn and reek of cancers

For a thousand years

And a thousand more

Thou shall be observed with aqueous eyes

Examined from within

Enslaved by fluid

25

Premonitions

As dusk fell upon Divinity, darkness saturated the flooded streets, and the wind lashed the street lamps like dragon's breath. The rows of votive candles still burned, despite the church's gaping wound. The two remaining fluorescent bulbs swayed precariously over baby Jesus, illuminating the tear filled congregation. Mama was the strongest woman I knew, but I could feel her hand tremble in mine. Her moment of weakness, by all means, should have justified my fears, but there was a strange calmness residing deep inside of me, the likes of which I cannot explain. I wish I could have told her then, but I didn't understand it. I didn't understand any of it. Perhaps it was because I was only seven and there was still enough of a disconnect from reality that none of it seemed absolutely real. Perhaps it was something more.

Mama always said I would cry for no apparent reason when I was a little baby, and like clockwork, something threatening or bad would always follow: a stranger at the door, an unattended stove, an overflowing tub. Looking back, I should have seen it. I know I shouldn't blame myself, but sometimes I still do. A seven-year-old girl should never be granted that kind of burden, but all the warnings were there: The babel of neighborhood dogs echoing through the streets, the dying leaves that curled and shriveled before my eyes, the absence of song amidst the treetops, and of course, the dripping . . . the incessant dripping, that spoke only in my presence.

And then there were the clouds. Every little girl sees things in the clouds. But these were different. They seemed to loom over our house as I built sand castles underneath Mama's laundry line. The silky white sheets attempted to shroud me from their curious demeanor as they danced in the warm summer wind. It was as if I could almost reach out and touch them.

And of course, there was Moses, and the elusive flickering lights. But now, now there was something more. Something worse. The signs and premonitions were just the beginning - the tears were coming.

26

From Which Forth It Gushed

The wave hit like a freight train. The monster in the mirror shattered, launching sheets of shimmering glass into the darkening sky. The sea roared, and heartlessly separated the brother's fraternal embrace. The mass of water crushed them against the jagged framework as the water rose from the violent impact. Arman was launched from the east side of the architecture, and thrown into cushions of white water, sparing him from any lethal prominences. Sansar ascended the west side of the tower, his shoulder slammed the corner of the structure and immediately dislocated. The pain paled in comparison to the violent contractions of vomiting up salt water, and the terrifying fight for breath.

The monster resounded. A churning washing machine of currents poured over everything in its path. Arman was dragged under, as if something had pulled him down. Only the horrible muffle of thunder remained as his lungs screamed for air. His body churned head over heels, over and over, like an astronaut cut loose into the abyss of space. He could hear his own cries penetrate the dismal crush of water and began to let go of his life. The very moment he decided to breath the ocean into his lungs, his elbow shattered on the front grill of a 68 Skylark, sending his body over the hood and back to the surface. The roar of the deluge consumed his shrill, agonizing scream, and his yelps of agony fell upon deaf ears. Instinctively, he filled his lungs with as much precious O2 as he could store. Fearing he would go under at any second, he cried openly for his older brother.

The mass of unstoppable sea trod inland, echoing through the streets and buildings like a Boeing 747 flying directly overhead. As Sansar struggled to keep his head above the violent undertow, hoards of flailing bodies submerged all around him, some just out of arm's reach. He watched helplessly, as they pleaded with outstretched fingers, and disappeared into the depths of the demon's embrace.

Sansar was wise beyond his thirty-two years, possessed the ability to collect himself under unthinkable duress, and quickly shrugged it off. If anyone could survive such a cataclysm, it was Sansar - the quintessential pragmatist. He was already thinking ahead, in frames and snapshots, of what lay around each bend. The pain of his dislocation was unbearable, yet he refused to succumb to what lurked beneath. As he calculated the current and probable path of the iniquitous log flume, his eyes miraculously caught a glimpse of fine line, stretched across two buildings, glistening in the distance. He couldn't make out what it was, but knew it may be his only chance. The line became increasingly more visible with each subsequent gulp of salt water. A floral beach towel, a turquoise tank top, and a pair of khaki cargo shorts swayed precariously on the shimmering line, brazenly taunting the roaring rapids. It was then that the haunting realization set in - he was floating towards a series laundry lines that, in these neighborhoods, were generally drawn from second story windows.

The landscape suddenly shifted and the torrent doubled in velocity as it breached the foot of one of the steepest and longest hills in the valley. Sansar knew that a collision at the base of the hill would surely be fatal, or at the very least, break enough bones to prevent him from keeping his head above water. Overlook Blvd, known to the locals as Angels Cove, stretched a half mile into the heart of Seaside. People were known to hang their laundry and towels at the base of the hill with messages, such as *You Are Now Leaving Seaside* or *Come Again, Just Not Too Soon. We Need a Vacation Too,* strewn across their tapestries. Sansar was now at the mercy of the descent, yet miraculously the speed somehow contributed to his buoyancy, allowing him to keep sight of the lines. They were approaching much faster than he had prayed for, and yes . . . he was praying! I guess there's truth in the notion that even a godless man will find the Lord in a foxhole.

The lines shimmered in the distance, revealing a metallic glow, and of course, showcasing the inherent capability of slicing through flesh like potter's wire. The first line came into view. The line was taught, which he had hoped for. Thunder roared from the bottom of the cove, and he knew it was now or never. He gritted his teeth and reached out his arms with everything he had. The cartilage tore from his dislocated humerus as he wailed into the godless sky. His hands were cold and his grip weak, yet he managed to wrap them tightly around the cold steel line. The pegs instantaneously ripped from the window frames and scattered like shurikens, spinning in the mist, as he plummeted back into the sea.

The next line came quickly, teetering just beyond his reach. A dangling white towel with the words *In God We Trust* embroidered on its face, taunted him from above, as he passed scornfully underneath. He quickly vomited another gulp of salt water and braced himself for the next opportunity within the gauntlet of wires. He reached out, and once again, screamed in agony as he forced his fingers around the drenched rusted wire. Once again, the wire snapped and fell into the sea, along with the banner - *God Helps Those Who Help Themselves.*

As far as he could tell there were only two lines that lay between himself and sudden impact as he accelerated toward the base of the cove. The nearest was ornamented with several tapestries and tank tops hanging superfluously about the line. The final line flaunted a huge, solitary white banner traversing across its entirety. It would be his final chance.

The first line approached at breakneck speed, for none of the failed attempts even remotely slowed his trajectory. He locked onto the line like a hawk, despite his burning eyes. He knew this was it. A sharp flash of light shimmered from the line as he mustered up all reserves, and launched himself towards the elusive ligature. The cable glistened like fool's gold. "This is it," he thought to himself. "Divine intervention! God is finally revealing his mercy to me in a shimmer of light!" He reached out for the line with trust in his heart, and a tear in his eye, and embraced it with all he had. A sharp sting raced up his arm and the line was gone . . . and so was his finger. The deceitful hand of God was nothing more than thin steel piano wire strewn across two metal posts, and the shimmer of light was nothing more than a shimmer of light. The pain, however, was very real!

Determined to live, he collected himself once again, and focused on the encroaching distant banner, hanging like an angel in white. There would be no second chances. Like a ship upon a rocky shore, he would come to rest, and perish against the jagged stones of Angels Cove. With every heartbeat the line came closer into view. As the steel wire revealed its heavenly glory, his heart sank deep within his chest, for he realized the Line, his Saviour, was out of his grasp. All remnants of hope were shattered . . . or so he thought. The lone tapestry that hung from the glimmering line, lay suspended, an arm's length from the surface of the rising waters. The angel in white swayed seductively, just above the surface of the raging deluge, as it glistened in a solitary ray of heavenly light. A decorative weave of nautical rope ornamented the perimeter of the giant banner.

A flood of hope suddenly replaced the elder brother's utter

despair. He clenched his teeth and reached for the sky, screaming at the top of his lungs, as his shoulder ground bone to bone. He clutched the shoddy nautical rope with a nine-finger death grip. The giant tapestry swayed, and opened like a parasail, catching the updraft of the rushing water. The violent jolt ripped his bicep from the head of his humerus. The pain united with his shredded shoulder and severed finger, yet he managed to maintain his grip, despite the trinity of torment. The icy current tugged at his partially submerged lower limbs as he dangled helplessly from the tangled tapestry. He glanced up at his hand to assess the incessant stinging, only to realize there was only bone protruding from the medial portion of his hand where his pinky used to be. Drops of wine rained from his wrist, as he dangled precariously, in a virtual cruciform formation, over the raging highway of salt water, debris, and bloated bodies. He knew he could not hold on much longer due to the velocity of the water and the crushing pain. As he looked up toward the sky, beyond the protrusion of bone, and blood running down his arm, the entangled white angel presented herself to him, with the sweetest of biblical sentiments, etched into her ghostly white fabric,

> *My precious, precious child*
>
> *I love you and I would never leave you*
>
> *During your times of trial and suffering*
>
> *When you see only one set of footprints*
>
> *It was then that I carried you.*

Sansar mustered up a grateful smirk, and whispered to the heavens, "It's about fucking time!" The slighted tapestry ripped from the tattered nautical ropes, and he was back in the frigid sea.

27

The Book of Novus

It had been five long nights with minimal sleep. The poor old Englishman's eyes were as red as the frazzled bow tie beneath his chin. The text was becoming increasing more difficult to decipher. Its roots were weighted in unorthodox clusters of hieroglyphics and pseudo-Latin derivatives, but for the most part there was no rhyme or reason. Everything the tenacious little Englishman had deciphered thus far, spoke of things to come: omens, admonitions, extermination, eradication. Now something far more frightening presented itself from the dark dusty pages.

It spoke of properties and structures, mathematic configurations, and chemical compositions, all of which made very little sense when presented to a collected panel of the most esteemed and acclaimed physicists, mathematicians, chemists, kinesiologists, and physicians the world had to offer. The concepts were beyond earthly comprehension, and seemed to shamelessly transcend our finite intelligence. There was, however, a common factor or constant in the equation, an overarching theme of "transformation" apparent in a particular book, *The Book of Novus* - derivative of the Latin infinitive "novare" - to change or alter. The ancient papyrus sheets also made mention of "mutare" and "vicissitudo" - to mutate and change, respectively. Yet no concrete interpretation of the chapter could be made. The distraught old linguist's stomach tightened, and gurgled a groan of gastric acid, for he knew that although the words themselves were not completely discernible, the fabric from which they were woven was crystal clear. There were creatures amongst us that were capable of something we could not fully comprehend.

28

A Procession of Tears

I felt Mama's grip loosen on my wrist as Mrs. Hubble turned away, and dragged her herself back into the storm. The heavy wooden doors slammed shut, and there was silence.

"It's ok, sweetie. It's over now," Mama whispered.

"What's wrong with Mrs. Hubble, Mommy?"

"I don't know, sweetie. I don't know."

Mama sat down next to me and stared silently at the creaking wooden doors, along with the rest of the congregation. As I looked over, two teardrops washed down Mama's face, one within a fraction of a second from the other. As the wind toyed with the lock, I glimpsed over to the creaking wooden doors as well, fearing the bearer of bad news may return, but quickly dismissed it, as I was now fixated on something far more curious. This time I knew it was more than just a little girl's imagination. The tears rolled slowly down Mama's cheeks, circumnavigated, and came to rest just below her nose. The two teardrops anastomosed into one, rolled over her trembling lips, and fell to the floor. I watched in disbelief as the circumfused drops flowed up the incline of the central aisle towards the baptismal font. It seemed to elude everyone's radar but mine, as it slithered passes the lectern that once stood so majestically. All the while, the rain stained the tattered pages of the sacred book, as it sat helplessly on the drenched marble floor. The great dead oak lay strewn over the holy pages in an almost protective posture, like a charred, blackened beast protecting her young. The wind cried like ghostly children above our heads, and the gaping hole on the north wall that once bore a beautiful depiction of our Savior, was now reduced to nothing more than shards of stained glass.

Yet another teardrop fell from Mama's face, and hit the ground running. The moonlight from the rafters illuminated the curious droplet as it split into two separate entities upon impact. One trickled towards the altar, and the other crept under the two ominous creaking doors. A sudden silence consumed the church. The wind ceased and the rain abated. I remember thinking that was scarier than the storm itself. I could see the doors begin to shake as I watched from the solitude of my pew. Suddenly, the heavy wooden doors blew open, as if the storm had never subsided. A menacing outline of a man stood at the foot of the door, his ghostly silhouette preceded a darkening sky that seemed to herald the evils to come. All eyes were now fixated on the lanky figure that stood motionless in the shadow of the doorway. The heavy doors rocked in the wind, as the few remaining hinges creaked and swayed against the splintered frame. The figure in the doorway now commanded the attention of the entire congregation. The creature hobbled into the prevailing moonlight and revealed itself. It wasn't a creature at all! It was Mr. Wetherly. Or was it?

I knew Mr. Wetherly as the sweet old man who owned A Little Piece of Heaven, a quaint little antique shop on the outskirts of town. He would always pinch my cheeks and say, "How is my little angel today?" He would also talk Mama's ear off, probably because he was lonely in that little store all day without his beloved Agnes, who died in the shower a few years back. The poor old man found her there on the bathroom floor, halfway out of the stall.

Mr. Wetherly stood in the doorway, dressed in the same old tweed jacket, with the same old unruly grey hair, and the same old grey fedora. Everything about him looked like Mr. Wetherly, right down to his penny loafers. But something was wrong. I felt an unmistakable feeling of dread, something I had never felt in the presence of the polite old man before. I looked over at Mama, I could see it wasn't just me this time. When I looked back, his eyes were locked on mine. My heart began to pound in my chest, so loud I could feel it in my ears. I knew, with all my heart, that the man that stood before me was not Mr. Wetherly. When he finally looked away from me, Mama said reluctantly, "Mr. Wetherly, what is it? What's wrong?" The once genial old man stared stoically into the rafters as he watched the water trickle down the decomposing crucifix that hung above the altar. "They took her from me!" the man screamed, maintaining his gaze. "They took my beloved Agnes away from me!!!" I cried as the old man fell to his knees. He began to weep openly on the floor, and with his fingers interlocked, began to pray to the deteriorating effigy of Jesus,

Lord, save these children for they know not what is to come

They are no more than frightened sheep in the storm

They do not deserve such a fate

Father, they do not deserve such a fate!!!

The prayers suddenly stopped. The man's voice deepened to an almost unrecognizable timbre. The imploring tonality of his prayers slowly began to morph into some sort of maniacal ranting. He rocked back and forth on the floor like a possessed preacher uttering a dialect unrecognizable. Suddenly, the rocking stopped. The ranting ceased. It was silent, pin drop silent. The only sounds were those of the creaking rafters and trickling rain. I will never forget the sound that followed. A horrible, blood-curdling screech resounded from his lips and shattered the still of the air. It was the most horrific sound I had ever heard. I watched in horror as the entire congregation reflexively covered their ears and fell back into their seats. It sounded like a lamb being slaughtered at one hundred and ten decibels.

The darkness came over me once again, as Mama's hands covered my eyes. The terrifying wail suddenly silenced, and Mama's hands slowly peeled from my brow. Mr. Wetherly was dead. Yet another body stained the floor of the sacred sanctuary, and yet another nightmare was etched into my innocent seven-year-old mind.

29

Something Wicked This Way Comes

The old red pickup rocked rhythmically above the dusty city as her steamed windshield painted an opaque abstract of the city lights below. The view from the ledge was breathtaking. There was no Barry White, no Sade, or hypnotic sutra dance mix playing on the old rewired stereo; tonight's sultry soundtrack featured the warm whispering winds of summer backed by a symphony of crickets.

Billy and Sherry met back in high school and discovered the bluff shortly after graduation. Billy was twenty-one and Sherry just turned nineteen. Billy was thin and athletic, his face as chiseled as his abs. Sherry was a stunning Southern belle with gorgeous chestnut eyes, and the envy of every high school boy this side of Madison County.

"If we're all gonna die, might as well go out with a bang," Billy moaned with a mischievous grin. Billy pulled Sherry's head from his lap, and lifted her on top of him, high above the city lights. Sherry moaned into the night sky with no inhibition, for the night was theirs and theirs alone. Billy pulled her sexy brunette bob back as he slowly entered her, again and again. He reached his hands around the small of her back as she slowly gyrated, grazing her back against the steering wheel with every thrust. He cupped her perfect breasts in his hands and kissed her like she had never been kissed. Their lips smacked as she pulled away to moan, her perfect body arched over the steering wheel in the sweet Madison moonlight. Subtle drops of rain slowly began to caress the windshield as she ran her fingers through his short dark hair, threw his head back into the seat, and rode him faster and harder. Billy groaned with approval.

"I knew these head restraints would come in handy for something, baby," Billy panted as he wrapped his hands around her ass.

In a thrust of passion, Billy lifted her, and faced her towards the city lights, reverse cowboy style, "Ooh Billy, you're a wild man tonight," she giggled devilishly.

Billy bounced her off his lap, her perfect ass slapped against his tight abs. The playful drizzle on the windshield was now pounding on the roof.

"Billy! Billy! Don't stop!" Sherry begged.

Billy kissed her back just above her "just turned nineteen" butterfly tattoo and pushed her toward the windshield, "Baby, you are so fucking hot," he moaned as he admired the shape of her body in the light of the pale Madison moon.

In the heat of passion, Billy noticed that the water on the windshield had begun to bead. Too excited to care, he quickly chalked it up to a fresh coat of wax from last weekend's trip to the Wash and Stop. "Baby, don't stop! I'm almost there!" Sherry pleaded. Billy grabbed the nape of her neck and fucked her harder. The rain teamed down like tiny little creatures stomping angrily on the metal roof, as the wind began to moan, mocking the two young lovers.

Billy watched the water bead again, but this time, something was different. The drops suddenly disappeared from the windshield. The rain pounded the roof, yet not a single drop remained on the glass. The city lights became as clear as day, and so did the ghostly image in the distance.

"Fuck me, Billy. Fuck me! Don't you dare stop!" Sherry screamed.

"Fuck . . . me," Billy replied in a deeper than usual voice.

"Ooh, I love it when you talk dirty, baby. Don't stop!" Sherry moaned mischievously.

"Fuuck . . . Meee," Billy reiterated, elongating his vowels and abbreviating his manhood.

"Don't stop, baby! Why are you stopping!?" she pleaded, as she looked over her shoulder. Billy remained motionless, gazing into the distance through the steamed glass, uttering "fuck me" over and over again. Sherry turned to see what he could possibly be staring at to make him ignore his beautiful, horny girlfriend. She cleared the misty glass with her sweaty wrist and slowly spilled from his lap. A black funnel, a half-mile in diameter, inched its way towards the bluff as it devoured the city lights beneath them, the very city lights that they and their beloved families and friends called home.

30

Revelatio - The Final Chapter

"**D**ihydrogen monoxide, H20, a seemingly simple molecule," Mr. Lipman recalled from his early chemistry days, so many years ago. Two hydrogen atoms covalently bonded to a single oxygen atom create a dipole moment. Oxygen being more electronegative will attract the less electronegative atoms of neighboring water molecules. At least that is what we have believed to be gospel for all these years. The principles of physics we have sworn by, my good men, no longer seem to apply. I honestly don't know where to turn. No God? No Bible? No Physics? What next? No history? No dinosaurs? No man on the moon? I mean, I really don't know where to turn!"

"What are you getting at, sir?" the general inquired inquisitively. "What's with all the physics mumbo jumbo? I'm afraid you're gonna have to break it down for us, sir." Mr. Lipman poked his thick black frames towards the brim of his nose and navigated his finger back into the dark pages of the final chapter: *Revelatio*

For all thou hath perceived as truth

Shall be no more

Eyes shall be strung out

And plucked for crows to feed

"Dear God! The text speaks with a metaphoric tongue, but it is as clear as day! It's exactly what we've been seeing. Principles and scientific rules we have sworn by for centuries are being refuted.

Molecules are not behaving as they should. We have been living a faux reality, my friends. And now there is no time to study, or even comprehend the goings on of this all too apparent paradigm shift. Gentlemen, I am at a loss for words. I am afraid there is nothing more I can do here. The text has told me everything I need to know."

Mr. Lipman calmly rose to his feet, collected his thoughts, and addressed the panel with a stern, yet quivering brow, moments before finally reaching his breaking point, "Gentleman, this is not a war. Nor is it an acquisition of land. This is an extermination! Now I . . . I'm sorry. I really have to, I really must. I'm . . . I'm so sorry. I . . . I really must be going."

31

And on This Rock I Will Build My Church, and the Gates of Hell Shall Not Prevail Against It (Matthew 16:18)

Dr. Jenkins, a regular Sunday observer and long time staple of our congregation, pronounced Mr. William Wetherly dead at precisely 3 p.m. He knelt over his body in disbelief, and blessed him in the name of the Father, the Son, and the Holy Spirit. The good doctor was beside himself, for he had never seen anything like it, nor had any one of us. Something terrible had breached the sacredness of these four walls, and whatever it was wished its presence known. Tears fell from dismayed faces, and whispers cascaded over one another, creating an eerie white noise about the war torn sanctuary. Suddenly, Mrs. Olson began to sway back and forth. Her head smashed the edge of the sharp wooden pew as her body convulsed, and fell to the flooded church floor. Without hesitation, Mama ran over to help, along with everyone else. "Dear God, not another one," the good doctor exclaimed, as the dull thud shattered his gaze. He sprang up spritely, and ran over to Mrs. Olson, leaving the shell of Mr. Wetherly on the floor, eyes wide open, gazing up to the heavens, as though he were still alive.

And that's when I first saw it. I knew Mr. Wetherly was dead because Dr. Jenkins told us so, but while Mama was tending Mrs. Olsen, I swear I saw Mr. Wetherly wet his pants. Mama ran to my side the second she heard me scream. "What is it, baby!?" I lifted my arm and pointed at Mr. Wetherly as his bladder continued to empty over the floor. I vividly remember having this feeling, this terrible feeling, like I knew something awful was going to happen. I just knew. I can't really explain it. I never could. I looked up to the tattered statue of Jesus, as its head, bloodied by its thorny crown, gazed down with outcast arms, over Mr. Wetherly's evacuating corpse. I thought it was just urine at first, perhaps some sort of post-mortem reflex or muscular contraction. But it didn't stop. Then I noticed the two streams of tears that rolled from his shriveled face, and thought for sure he was still alive, that is, until his ears and mouth began to drain as well. Everyone just stood there, entranced. I think everyone was in shock, even Mama, cause she forgot to cover my eyes. Every orifice of his body soon began to discharge fluid. His pores oozed from head to toe, saturating his white shirt and dress pants, as though his body was in a state of purification or purgation. The discharge turned red. Blood hemorrhaged from his eyes, ears, and mouth, even the underside of his fingernails were not exempt from the crimson crusade. Suddenly a bloody stream burst from between his legs, and the darkness was upon me. Mama clutched me in her arms and shielded my eyes from the horror that was happening before us.

And that's when I heard it. That's when we all heard it. A horrible, loud pop, like a giant water balloon had just burst. Everyone screamed in unison at the top of their lungs. I felt Mama's sheltering hands leave my eyes as she fell to her knees and vomited at my feet. When I looked up, everyone was covered in blood. A sea of sanguine stained the floor where Mr. Wetherly once lay. The majority of the congregation fell to their knees and joined Mama on the floor.

I must have been in shock or something because everything seemed to move in slow motion, except for me. If anything, my senses seemed heightened, finely tuned. It was like my nerves were on the outside of my skin. No one even noticed the torrent of body fluids congealing and flowing up stream towards the altar. The alien river bled out, center stage, just beyond the pulpit. Its mass now appeared to be clear, as though the blood and urine it had discarded, had been filtered out or metabolized. Holy water spilled from every urn. As it flowed towards the altar in a hesitant procession, it congealed with the puddle of alien bile, completing the unholy union. I watched curiously as the translucent force began to take shape, rising towards the rafters. Its crude form continued to refine itself, revealing the shape of a formidable, almost human-like figure. I couldn't look away. I just stood there staring straight at it.

The gates of hell had opened, and my premonition of dread was now taking life, just beyond the altar. I slowly reached over and tapped Mama on the head without ever so much as blinking. Mama wiped her mouth and struggled to her feet, "Christy? What's wrong, baby?" I slowly raised my arm and pointed towards the altar. Mama's eyes followed my finger to the unholy creation twitching in the dull light. Her handbag fell to the floor with a thud, and the room went silent, dead silent.

32

Let Thy Fountains be Dispersed Abroad, and Rivers of Waters in the Streets (Proverbs 5:16)

"You know, Mikey, this shit makes perfect sense now! All those times you beg God to help you out, you get nothin'. Or you beg him to not let somethin' happen, and it happens. Then you fucking feel guilty for doubting his existence! Can you believe that shit!? I gotta feel guilty for doubting the existence of something that supposedly created me? What a fucking joke! Yep, it all makes sense now, my friend. We were just some pathetic experiment created to entertain these fuckers, and that's why we never got anything from "Mr. Almighty" . . . 'cause he never fucking existed!"

Mike Bruzzi and Tony Bellucci had been next-door neighbors for twenty years now. The kids grew up together and Rosanne and Marie were the best of friends.

"I hear what you're saying, Tony. I'm all fucked up over this shit too. Listen, take a walk, will ya? Let's go out in the street, the kids don't need to hear this crap."

"Yeah, you're right, Mikey. Good idea." Tony looked the old neighborhood up and down and shook his head in disgust, "Look at this place, Mikey. It's like a fucking ghost town. Everybody's scared to even come outta their own homes. If I could get my hands on one of these fuckers, I'd fuckin' smack it around. You know what I mean?"

Mikey slicked his dark Sicilian hair back and vigilantly scoured the ghostly haven, "Yeah, I wouldn't mind taking a bat upside some alien head myself".

Tony put his hand on Mikey's lanky shoulder, looked at him with the sincerity of a saint, and gave him the old gentle Italian cheek slap, "You know you're like a brother to me, right? You know that? And we ain't gonna let nothin' happen to our families, capeesh? I love ya, you big Mamaloot."

Tony was a big boy, weighing in at close to 250 lbs. He was of Sicilian descent as well, but had slightly less hair than Mikey. He served in the Marine Corps in his youth, until his knee gave out on him about ten years ago, but still wears the ink proudly on his arm. Mikey never saw Tony cry, not in twenty years, but the sight of it got Mikey started with the water works. And there they were, two tough-ass paisans bawling in the deserted streets of Suburbia, "I love ya too," Mikey requited with a loving cheek smack, "Now cut the shit, before I take a baseball bat to you instead! Besides, it's gettin' late. We better get inside before the wives think we're up to no good."

No sooner than the two goombahs departed the desolate street, the very street that once echoed with the sound of children's laughter, did the real waterworks begin. Every fire hydrant on Maple Street burst, in an eerie synchronous blast, spraying fountains of water a hundred feet into the sky. A conspiracy of fluid flooded the neighborhood in a matter of seconds. Suddenly the ghost town was alive, with curious bystanders, families, children, all watching the fountains rain into their front yards. Tony and Mikey were amongst the curious, and watched the columns of water tower over the houses like sentries.

"Holy shit!!! Are you seeing this, Mikey?" Tony pointed to the rooftops of the houses on the other side of the street, "It's not just us! It's happening on Shadyside and Sandy court!"

Mikey hesitantly turned around, "Fuck me! Looks like Salem's gettin' hit too!" Suddenly the sound of rotor blades crescendoed overhead, as a trio of choppers scoured the surrounding neighborhood with spotlights and megaphones, GET BACK IN YOUR HOUSES IMMEDIATELY. THIS IS NOT A DRILL. I REPEAT . . . THIS IS NOT A DRILL. The rotor blades churned the sheets of mist into swirling entities that seemed to momentarily take shape and dissipate back into the atmosphere.

"Ain't this some shit, Mikey? The brass up in D.C. can't even keep the water companies from blowin' their lids, and now they want us locked up in our own homes? Screw them! I'll stand in my front friggin' yard if I want to! Ain't that right, Mikey?"

"Uh, I don't know, Tony. Somethin's not right about this. Maybe we should listen."

"Screw them, Mikey. They're not lockin' me in my own home unless there's some sorta plague goin' round. For Christ's sake, it's just water!"

33

When the Bow Breaks the Cradle Will Fall

He dropped like a soiled shirt, back into the spin cycle. The icy water sprayed the blood from his face as he choked on the filthy sea. Sansar had evaded the bone crushing impact at the bottom of Angel's Cove but was now at the mercy of the winding labyrinth of twists and turns knows as In Valle Serpentes - The Valley of The Serpents.

Unbeknownst to his elder brother, Arman was simultaneously touring the outskirts of hell himself. Despite his thirty plus hours of swim lessons and endless words of encouragement from his beloved mother, Arman was weak and lacked the physicality of his elder brother. He struggled to keep from going under with every bombastic, agonizing stroke. The waters churned like Charybdis, taunting him like a helpless sailor, entrapped in her web of whirlpools. The crush of ocean spared nothing, collecting everything in its opposing path: streetcars, storefronts, even the telephone lines snapped like pretzel sticks. The only formidable adversaries, it seemed, were the pliable California pines that adorned the boulevards. The surviving greens jetted out above the sea of white foam, swaying precariously close to the surface, taunting and teasing, as they stood victoriously. Arman desperately clawed for anything to grab onto, for the will to carry on was leaving him, "I don't want to die!!!" he cried aloud, but quickly stifled his sobbing, for he knew he would swallow more of the vile sea. "Dear God, please help me!!! I beg you!!! Spare me, so I may see my brother again!" he prayed as the sea whisked him around the sharp corners of the storefronts, slicing his external oblique open like a razor. The sting of salt burned him like the thorny barbs of hell, yet something told him to hold on just a little bit longer.

As his face breached the surface, he spotted a lone pine, lurched over, swaying in a lull of currents at the base of Azrael's fall, the steepest incline in the valley. Arman reached out frantically, and miraculously latched on to the arcing pine. She gently cradled him into the foliage of her matronly embrace. He nuzzled up to her bow like a newborn king to Mother Mary, and climbed as far as he could before his burden caused her crown to arc back towards the sea. Despite sitting a mere ten feet above the roaring rapids, he gasped a breath of sweet relief, for his prayers had been answered. "Blessed art thou among women", he whispered to the matronly tree. He draped himself over her bowing shoulder like a veil as her body began to arch, allowing him to rest his weary arms and legs, which were now reduced to waterlogged limp noodles.

The relentless rush of ocean suddenly began to abate, and transformed itself into a constant glass like state. The fury of the wave had finally reached its apogee. Or had it?

Arman took a deep breath and surveyed the land, or lack thereof, for he could not believe his burning eyes. The still of the water revealed a creaking watery graveyard. Bodies flowed underneath him, some face up with frozen stares. As the bodies floated passed him in a sickening aquatic funeral procession, Arman wept uncontrollably, almost falling from his nest. He thought of Sansar, and feared he may be next in the procession. "My God!" he professed, "I do not understand your logic, yet I shall not believe what I hear, nor shall I forsake thee." Suddenly a mysterious figure drifted toward him from the distance. It was a man who appeared to be lying supine on a bevy of boards. The ghostly figure in the distance slowly began to come into focus. He was a tall man, with dark hair, a dark complexion, and "Dear God, please don't do this to me!" Arman begged. The lifeless entangled figure materialized before his eyes. He cried and begged apprehensively, "Sansar?! Please God!" The body lay upon a bed of boards, aligned in a happenstance crucifix formation, as it washed underneath him. Arman gasped, and bellowed a cry of sweet relief. The drowned soul draped over the reaper's raft would not be his beloved brother, but judging from the tool belt hanging from his bloated torso, an unfortunate carpenter swept away by an unforgiving sea.

34

The Devil and the Deep Blue Sea

The encroaching black funnel slithered through Madison County as Billy and Sherry scrambled from the truck. "Jesus Christ, that's an easy F4!" Billy uttered, as they stood half naked, witnessing the devastation from atop the bluff. "They didn't even have a chance! It was like it just dropped out of the sky!"

They stood like statues high above the city lights, transfixed, as the black demon devoured and spit out everything in its path, "Billy, we have to do something! My parents, your parents, everyone we love is down there!"

Billy gazed into her welling eyes, "Get in the truck."

He tore up the old trails, gunning it down the mountain like a bat out of hell. The 350 hemi squealed like a wild boar as it rounded each muddied turn. "Get out of the way!" he screamed, as the columns of townsfolk lined the edge of the road and stared like zombies at the infringing serpent. Billy was halfway down the mountain when Sherry noticed the funnel beginning to shift. It was hard to be certain due to its hypnotic demeanor and monstrous girth, but is was indeed shifting. It was headed straight toward the old red Chevy as it careened down the side of the mountain.

The road itself was a roll of the dice, bluff on one side, rock on the other. There was nowhere to go but down, and Billy was gunning it between the devil and the deep blue sea, trying not to kill them both in the process. The intent of the whimsical beast was now crystal clear. Sherry screamed hysterically, "Billy! It's coming towards us!! It's coming towards us!!!" Billy jammed the brakes. The truck slid sideways, throwing mud and stone over the edge as it fishtailed out of control. Billy gripped the wheel so tightly he almost ripped it from the dash.

The truck finally came to rest, an arms length from the edge of the cliff wall. A large boulder lodged itself underneath the front axel as the incapacitated tire spun freely, squeaking like a mouse on the cat's tongue. The black funnel ripped into the rock wall about a half-mile up as it sandblasted the edge of the mountain, pulling everything in its vicinity closer to the edge, including Billy and Sherry. Boulders from the adjacent rock wall shifted, and bowled down the embankment, missing the truck by inches. "Son of a bitch!!" Billy shouted as one smashed down into the bed of the pickup. They both watched in horror as homes, trees, and anything that wasn't bolted down was sucked off the edge of the bluff.

Then, as quickly as the serpent reared its ugly head, it was gone. The squeals subsided and the funnel evanesced as it collided with the mountain, severing its heavenly connection to Mother Earth. The churning beast was dead. Sherry reached for the door handle. Billy quickly grabbed her hand, "Not yet, baby." He studied the deceiving sky, "It may be back burning." They sat silently, scouring the night sky as debris rained down all around them. Suddenly the keys in the ignition began to jingle. They looked at each other simultaneously, confirming what the other was thinking.

The earth began to shake and the sickening roar resumed, "Is it back!? I don't see it!" Sherry cried.

Billy looked in the rearview and noticed stones raining onto the road. He poked his head out the driver's side window and looked up, "Son of a . . . HOLD ON!!!" The tattered rock wall that towered above them gave way and crumbled. A renegade of rocks and boulders slammed the pick up, spinning it on its axis and pushing the front end over the bluff. The truck teetered on the edge like a seesaw, high above the city lights; the boulder in its bed, its solitary saving grace. The angry wind downgraded to a gentle breath upon the mountain's torn and tattered cheek. The only sounds to be heard were the groans of the wounded pickup, precariously rocking and creaking, a half-mile above the lonesome city lights of a bleeding city.

35

In This House No Butterfly Shall Dwell

The eerie still of the church was shattered by the sound of the metamorphosis attempting to free itself from its unearthly cocoon. It shook and shuddered violently, emitting a deafening squeal, resembling that of Mr. Wetherly, a screeching cat, and God knows what else. Whatever it was, it rose from infernal origin and spoke with an unholy tongue. The anthropomorphous figure emitted a putrid odor as it began to take shape, recycling Mrs. Olson's altar bound fluids to further solidify its form. A strange viscous fluid flowed through its transparency, maintaining constant motion, like thousands of translucent snakes slithering through its anatomy, or lack thereof.

Mrs. Catalano, a heavy set Czech woman, slowly rose to her feet, "What is it you want from us!?" she demanded. The ghostly figure remained unresponsive, slithering in its shell. "DAMMIT, ANSWER ME!" she screamed at the top of her voice. Mr. Catalano grasped his wife's hand to stop her from inching any closer to the bizarre mutating entity, "Honey, no!" he whispered under his breath. The creature reared its head towards the perceived threat edging its way towards the altar. The aqueous intruder lifted a watery limb towards the intrepid woman and her sheepish pleading husband. Before I could even blink, Mrs. Catalano was reduced to a biliary puddle of ooze, right before my disbelieving eyes, leaving her cowering husband on the floor, in a ball of shock, drenched in her remains.

Shrieks of terror reverberated off the ecclesiastical architecture, appearing to alarm the demoniacal force. The creature pointed, with its fluid-filled phalanx, just as it did with Mrs. Catalano, beyond the broken stained glass, and out towards the largest tree in the courtyard. The giant oak turned black, and rotted from the inside out, just as I had witnessed before, only this time the blight infected the base only, sparing the heavy upper limbs.

The monster oak toppled onto the church, barring the front doors from the onslaught of hysterical screaming parishioners. In one fell swoop, Mama grabbed me by the waist, and with one arm, scooped me up like a rag doll. I watched the volatile figure sway from side to side, from over her shoulder, as she whisked me toward the back of the church. I remember looking around and seeing all the other kids hoisted upon their parent's shoulders as well, and wondered why the church floor was suddenly submerged under several inches of water. And then I realized. My perspective of the altar became infinitely clearer with each one of Mama's retreating, sloshing steps. Fluid emptied from the base of the creature, encircling us all in a web of ooze. I looked around the room and all the kids were crying, clinging to their parent's necks. Every single one of them! Why was I not scared? Why was I not crying? What the hell was wrong with me? Outside, the darkening skies belched buckets, infecting the church's gaping wound, while the menacing green nimbus clouds created an eerie backdrop that seemed to herald the end of the world . . . And yet I was not afraid.

36

Out of His Belly Shall Flow Rivers of Living Water (John 7:38)

"Jesus, Mikey, a little water never hurt no one. I mean seriously, what's a matter for you? You afraid of a little water?" It was more than a little water . . . much more. Something sinister had found its way into the peaceful suburb of Hallow Pines.

Tony finally surrendered to logic when he heard the sirens and screams radiating from within the neighborhood, "Mikey, grab Marie and the kids, and come in with us."

Mikey conceded with a quick nod. "Marie, grab Joey and Belle, we're going next door!" Tony grabbed his arm as he was leaving, "And Mikey, grab your rifle, and as many shells as you can stash." Mikey nodded once again.

"Roseanne, get Angela and lock the back door."

"Tony, what's happening?!"

"I don't know, baby, just get Angela and lock the back door." Mikey and Marie corralled the kids and hightailed it next door.

"C'mon! C'mon! Get your asses in here already. Mikey, lock the door, will ya?"

"Roseanne, what is going on?" Marie asked anxiously.

"I have no idea! Tony said the fire hydrants are bursting all over the place! That's all I know!"

Dusk approached quickly, and Hallow Pines unwillingly succumbed to the darkness. Lights flickered like fire flies as the neighborhood faded into the shadows. A commotion at the end of the block peaked Tony's curiosity. He separated the blinds with his finger and surveyed the lonely streets. He could barely make out the man on the corner through the haze of hydrants and darkening skies, "My God, is that Carl?" he whispered to himself. Suddenly, the man on the lawn collapsed onto his knees and screamed into the heavens. The heart wrenching cries resonated half way up the block and permeated the fogged glass. As Tony brushed his bewildered brow, a bevy of black uniforms lined up, single file, and locked their rifles on the man. Or so it seemed. Tony could barely make it out, but something large stood over the distraught sobbing man. The black uniforms opened fire in a controlled burst.

"Jesus Christ!" Tony whispered as he stepped back from the window, fearing he had just witnessed an execution.

"Tony, what is happening!?" Roseanne cried.

He reluctantly fingered the blinds open once again. Every single black uniform lay on the floor, twitching and jerking. And suddenly they were still. The mysterious man on the lawn remained, screaming bloody murder into the darkening sky, seemingly unaffected by the gunshots and writhing black uniforms. Tony inched away from the window and said nothing. The ghostly silhouette that lurked above the frenetic man on the corner, crumbled to the ground and invaded the orifices of the five black uniforms, drowning the men where they stood, all of which evaded Tony's view, amidst the curtain of mist and darkness.

"Tony, what is it!?" Roseanne demanded, as she clutched Angela tightly in her arms.

"I have no fucking clue, Roseanne," he muttered as he stared at the misty window, "No fucking clue."

As Tony fingered the blinds open one last time to try and make sense of the bizarre sequence of events that had just unfolded before his eyes, something presented itself outside the fogged glass. It peered up at him and vanished into the hedges, depositing a dripping ooze on the rustling bush below.

Tony jumped back from the window, "Son of a . . . what the fuck!!!?" He quickly closed the curtains and slowly backed away, "Mikey, grab your fucking rifle!"

"Daddy, I'm scared," Joey cried.

Mikey knelt down beside him while Belle stood quietly embraced in her mother's arms, "Joey, look at me. It's gonna be ok, I promise. Marie, take Joey, please."

Tony stood vigilantly, eyeing the vicinity of the living room, "Roe, you locked all the doors, right?"

A tear streamed down her cheek as she nodded up and down, and yet another ghostly figure brushed by the adjacent window, "Son of a Bitch! Mikey, give me a hand, quick!" They quickly dragged the couch across the room and barricaded the front door.

"What the hell are those things, Tony? I keep seeing shit out there!"

"I don't know, Mikey, but whatever the fuck they are, they ain't gettin' in here unless they wanna get popped."

Tony looked over his shoulder, "Roseanne, Marie, grab the kids. Everyone get in the middle of the room. We got two doors here. We're gonna need more than one pair of eyes."

They all stood in the center of the room, like sheep in a pen, awaiting the wolf in the woods. Armed sheep! All eyes shifted from the front door - to the side door - and back again. Mikey had his rifle cocked and slated on the side door, while Tony manned the front entrance. The distant screams were becoming more consistent, and getting closer by the minute. Something scurried past the bush and made its way onto the stoop, faintly revealing itself through the distorted kaleidoscope windows on the side door. The doorknob began to jiggle and Mikey cocked his 22. A horrible gurgling noise filled the hallway as a body fell to the floor and slapped the pavement. Tony ran to the window, his rifle leading the way. Mikey trailed cautiously, his rifle also leading the way. It was Mrs. Ravini from next door. Tony opened the door vigilantly, and quickly pulled her inside.

"My God, is she alive?" Roseanne cried from the center of the living room as she shielded Angela's eyes from the site of the woman sprawled out upon the kitchen floor.

Tony knew right away she was gone, "Stay in the room, Roe!" Fluid oozed from every orifice, and her body reeked of a putrid, unrecognizable odor. All eyes were on the kitchen entrance, awaiting some sort of explanation as to what the hell had just happened. All eyes, that is, except for little Belle's. She stared at the strange man in the living room that seeped underneath the front door during the commotion.

A cacophony of flickering lights, high-pitched pops, and agonizing screams corroded the outside world, as the neighborhood homes dimmed one by one. The Bellucci house was not exempt. The lights flickered and the house went black. Screams emanated from the center of the room. Tony and Mikey stumbled in at the mercy of the darkness. A strange buzz preceded a rapid flicker, and the lights were on again. And there stood whatever the hell it was that Belle was so intrigued by. Tony blasted into the center of it. Whatever is was burst and fell into a puddle upon the living room floor. The fluid seemed to multiply, saturating the flickering room.

The house buzzed and went black once again, as Tony waded ankle deep in the darkness. This time there were no screams coming from the center of the room. Tony raised his rifle, threatened by the deafening silence. Hyperventilation and the pounding of his chest made it hard to steady the barrel. A chilling thirty seconds elapsed, and the lights flickered on for the last time. "Dear God!" Tony whispered, as he slowly lowered his rifle to the floor, which was now curiously bone dry. There stood his beloved wife, his beautiful daughter, Mikey, Marie, Belle, and Joey, with their backs up against the living room wall. Terror was etched on each of their faces, yet they could not speak. A single chain of fluid coiled around each of their necks like a serpent. Its head wrapped around the base of the steel radiator pipes, and its tail dangled tauntingly over the electrical outlet above Tony's favorite armchair, like a translucent scorpion. The lights flickered and the scorpion inserted its tail. A sickening pop preceded a burst of blue light that lit up the watery chain of bondage like blue garland.

Their screams were concise and gargled. Five bodies slammed to the floor and the desecrated house went black. The last sound that was ever heard from 51 Pine Street was the sound of a 22 blowing off the bottom of Tony Bellucci's jaw.

37

The Lord Giveth, and The Lord Taketh Away (Job 1:21)

Sansar poured through the twists and turns of Serpents Valley like a steel ball racking up points on a permeable, perverse pinball machine. The only difference - bumpers were buildings, and buzzers and bells screams of agony. His mangled shoulder tore with each successive impact, as the saliferous sea gnawed at his bloody stump. The blood loss was beginning to take its toll. The streets were now literal floating parking lots, so thick with death and debris, one could almost walk on water. Sansar careened off a '78 Maverick, then sideswiped a '57 Charger, racking up 135 bonus points on the barbarous Bally table. He proceeded to thread the needle between a '72 Cargo Van and a Celebrity Tour Bus, evading the "Malachi Crunch" for the win. Suddenly the current began to mitigate. The relentless forward motion of the locomotive had reached its final stop. All was still. An eerie silence consumed the air for the first time since the killer wave struck the coastline. A stray boardwalk piling crept up from behind, lightly nudged him, and invited him aboard. He graciously accepted, and exhaled, as the horrifying realization of just how far he had traveled inland weighed on his weary mind. He bowed his head, cradled his face in his bloodied hands, and whispered aloud, "Thank you, Lord." The songs of the circling gulls soothed his wilted soul, as they monopolized on the displaced sea bass tossed upon the rooftops. Soon the crows joined the choir, yet their song was not sweet, for they feasted upon the dead.

As he laid his head upon his splintered pillow, the comforting cries of the gulls began to sound more human-like. The distant bellows from inland tangled with the birds, creating an unnerving crescendoing squalor. He felt a slight pull at his feet, as they dangled in the stagnant sea, and realized the screams were indeed human, and undeniably growing louder. And immediately he knew, "Dear God, it's receding!!!" A sickening symphony of scraping metal and cracking wood ensued as the receding ocean began to collect all it had taken. Sansar latched onto his pilling, tooth and nail, and braced himself for the worst. The angry sea was retreating, coveting everything in its path, and Sansar was in the midst of the thickening soup.

Arman, unbeknownst to his beloved brother, lay nestled atop his savior, the redeeming swaying pine, a mere two blocks away. As he lay there, the unfortunate carpenter on the reaper's raft returned, and floated underneath the sacred pine once again. This time, the ghostly corpse was not alone. A fifty-foot utility pole followed in its wake, slamming the arched pine from behind, launching Arman, like a catapult, back into the frigid sea. He plunged face first, back into the debris-laden cavalcade, spitting out two teeth and a mouthful of blood, as his jaw slammed the protruding bumper of a partially submerged yellow cab. The heterogeneous mixture creaked and clanged as the solid mass consumed him. The velocity of the recession intensified as it reunited with the descending landscape. The water flowed swiftly, yet silently, accumulating everything it had ravaged, leaving Arman the pick of the litter in flotation devices. The hard part was hanging onto any given object without being crushed or drowned by the surrounding debris.

After countless failed attempts, Arman latched onto a beat up cooler floating amidst the trees and logs, of which were too risky of an endeavor to crawl upon. Out of the corner of his eye emerged a

'62 pink VW Bug, closing in from behind. He thought to himself, "Thank you, Lord, for letting her be a pink Bug and not a yellow fucking school bus!" Her nose shoveled the surface like a submarine and slammed the cooler head on, scooping him atop her arced chassis. He sank his fingers into the lip of the roof where the windshield used to be, secured himself, and graciously exhaled.

As he lay strewn over her convex canopy, utterly exhausted, his eyes scathing and stinging from the salt, a ten-foot streak of gray and white breached the surface, about fifteen-meters ahead, thrashed about for an instant, and submerged. Arman, too tired to even care, pondered to himself, as his eyes glazed over, "Nah . . . couldn't be."

38

Lipman's Last Stand

My fellow Americans! Ladies and Gentlemen of the jury! This shall be my final translation for you all, frankly because I am fed up with this bloody shitting book. Forgive my lack of linguistic prowess, but I have been drowning my sorrows in, let us call it, the good ol' well of iniquity, which has bestowed to me a lovely 50 yr old scotch!

So what has this godforsaken book been trying to tell us, you ask? Well I'll tell you, my fellow pawns and confidants. Basically gentlemen, we are fucked, that's what it says! A long long time ago when the Earth was dormant and yearning for life . . . blah blah blah, within her womb a seed shall be planted . . . blah blah blah! And to the womb ye shall return. How original! How poetic! Yet another pompous pissing metaphor about death, and returning to the soil of good ol' Mother Earth! They can kiss my drunken British ass!

Hmm . . . what other tasty tidbits may I amuse ye with, my curious little kittens. Oh yes, it seems we are no more than, pointless, pathetic prototypes made up of arbitrary cells. Arbitrary cells! Simply stated, we have been branded as simpletons for believing we were once conceived from the rib of man. Come to think of it, maybe those wily, facetious, little bastards have a point! It is quite ludicrous, indeed!

Oh yes, and it seems we simply cannot keep it in our pants, and cease to procreate, despite mutation, maldevelopment, disease, and all the other lovely afflictions we have been blessed with. And If that doesn't float your arc, then how is this for a loving final sentiment . . . Just as it was in the beginning, the Earth shall be deemed silent, once again, and all life shall cease, and soil the dust from whence it came.

Soooo . . . to recapitulate, my unworthy and meek comrades, we are totally fucked! Let us heed the prophetic words of the "Good Book", and I quote, 'Put on the whole armour of God, that ye may be able to stand against the wiles of the Devil.' (Ephesians 6:11)

I love you all, and it has been a pleasure serving with you. This is your friendly neighborhood linguist signing off. May our fictitious God have mercy on our fictitious souls. Good luck, my dear friends. I love you all.

Sent from my iPad

39

A Noble Mind No More

The church filled with fluid as I sat upon Mama's shoulder. Panic proliferated the pews as parishioners clutched on to one another like rats trapped in a filling sewer grate. No one knew what the hell was happening. Suddenly, as I sat perched above the pandemonium, the feeling came over me like a fever. My little heart pounded, and the sweat beaded on my forehead. My insides began to tingle, as blood ran rabid through my veins. My pupils dilated, and the hairs on my arms stood on edge. I suddenly possessed the ability to see images from very far away, and could hear a pin drop at a hundred meters.

A distant light shone through the framework of the shattered stained glass window. It was Brady's Appliance Store, which sat high upon the hill, and overlooked the church, about a half- mile down the road. I could see it clear as day. A lone big screen TV, that had mysteriously survived the onslaught of rioters, illuminated through the shattered storefront window. A cryptic message slowly scrolled down the flickering screen,

>*A long long time ago*
>
>*The Earth lay silent, dormant, yearning for life*
>
>*And within her womb, a seed was planted*
>
>*And the seed, it did bare fruit*
>
>*Prototypical, pointless, pathetic fruit*

A mindless genus derived from arbitrary cell structures

Capable of being deceived

Hence, conception, bestowed by the rib of man

A strain far too fertile to cease procreation

Despite mutation, blight, and disease.

Behold, just as it was in the beginning

The Earth shall be deemed silent, once again

And to the womb ye shall return

And all life, big and small, shall cease

And soil the dust from whence it came.

A disheveled man with tears in his eyes appeared on the flittering screen, "My friends, this appears to be the final translation of *Revalatio*. It is with great sadness I inform you, that at approximately 1 a.m. this morning, my dear dear friend Ernest Lipman took his own life." A long moment of dead air ensued as the distraught man tried to regain his composure. "I am afraid I have more terrible news," he whimpered, barely able to contain himself. "I have just been informed that the President of the United States, the first lady, and their beloved children are gone. I repeat . . . the President and his family are dead!" The luminous screen flickered intermittently, spewing fragments of information between interference. "Their bodies were found hand in hand, strewn across the flooded White House floor. The apparent cause of death was said to be electrocution."

The visualization of the first family laid out on the floor was too much for the broadcaster to bear. He sobbed uncontrollably, "I'm sorry! We have lost our commander-in-chief and his beautiful family, and God knows how many others! I pray for you all, and your families!"

A long moment of dead air elapsed, and the screen burst into static. And suddenly I was back in the church, in the midst of the chaos. I was scared for the very first time, truly scared. Not for me, but for everyone else, for I knew what was to come.

40

A False Balance Is Abomination to the Lord: But a Just Weight Is His Delight (Proverbs 11:1)

The city lights of Madison beckoned below as the tattered truck creaked on the edge of the bluff. The dimming headlights captured the dust in their beams as they shone out into the night sky. "Lean back as far as you can against the seat!" Billy exclaimed in a moment of pseudo composure. The two young lovers instantaneously glued themselves to the seats, gasping as they gazed into the abyss below. The truck stabilized, but only for the moment. The cliff wall was slowly giving way as the weight of the truck and surrounding boulders settled. The tattered rock wall behind them rumbled in the distance, temporarily bridling its potential energy. Billy reached over his shoulder ever so slowly, and toggled the rear window latch that opened to the bed of the truck,

"Baby, listen to me," Billy whispered. "I'm gonna crawl out the back and pull you through."

"NOOO, don't move!!!" Sherry pleaded. Billy knew her fear of heights was consuming her; she was shaking so hard the screws in the cup holder were coming loose.

Billy put his finger over her mouth, "Listen to me, baby. Stay wedged up against the seat! We're getting out of here, ok? Look at me, Sherry." Sherry shifted her eyes without moving her neck.

"Ok!?" Billy whispered emphatically.

"Oh oh oh kay," Sherry cried under her breath, trembling and barely able to speak.

Billy arched his way up and over the seat, and slowly muscled his way into the bed of the old pickup. He glanced quickly at the shivering rock wall towering above them and knew it wouldn't be long. He sprawled his legs out towards the back of the truck and reached into the cab, "Take my hand, baby." Sherry was unresponsive, her body paralyzed with fear. And the birds eye view of the 3/4 mile vertical drop wasn't helping. Billy could hear the rumbling from behind intensify. "Baby, listen to me. Close your eyes and give me your hand. I will do the rest. Just give me your hand." The rumbling was peaking, and he prayed with all his heart she couldn't hear it. "C'mon, baby. You can do this! I got you!" he whispered. Sherry slowly reached out her shaking hand. Billy latched on with everything he had and pulled her up towards the window. "You're almost there, baby, you're almost there." Suddenly, she was dead weight. Her sneaker lace had wrapped itself around the gearshift. "Lift your left leg, baby," Billy whispered calmly. She lifted her right. "Your other left, baby."

The trembling wall of stone gave way. The aggregate wave thundered towards the dangling red truck. "LEFT!!! LEFT!!! LEFT!!!" Sherry flailed both of her legs in despair, miraculously freeing her left. Billy yanked her through the window with all his might. She shrieked in pain as her body slapped the rusty bed of the pickup like a snapper freed from a fisherman's line. A boulder the size of a Buick led the exodus of dangling disciples down the hill. "JUMP!!!!" Billy screamed as they clumsily stumbled to their feet in the bed of the doomed Chevy. Billy shoved Sherry out of the truck an instant before he leapt, assuring she was clear of the stampede. The first boulder in the procession clipped his leg, shattering his tibia, as he leapt to her side. The renegade of rock plucked the pickup from the edge like a murder of crows, and from its angry talons, released it into the depths of the desolated city below. And she was gone. The dust settled, as an ebony cloud rose up the top of the bluff where Billy and Sherry lay in a puddle of antifreeze and rubble.

"We made it, baby," Billy whispered, laboring a painful smile, as he stared down at the fiery wreckage.

The look of assurance in Sherry's eyes was suddenly eclipsed by a black veil of fear, "Billy!?" Sherry watched as a green noose of fluid insidiously coiled around his neck. One end constricted his trachea causing him to gasp for air, as the other end forced itself into his mouth. Sherry screamed in horror and reflexively pulled the aqueous serpent from his neck. Billy stumbled to his feet, frantically wiping his mouth, "Son of a bitch! What the fuck was that!?" he screamed as he vomited antifreeze.

They slowly backed away from the slithering puddle and simultaneously gave it the finger. Billy wrapped his arm around Sherry's neck as they began to hobble down the trail, back to the ravaged town they once called home. Billy kissed her on the cheek as they limped away, "Motherfucker! . . . good thing I used a 50:50 ratio!"

41

For Thee Who Taketh Thy Bone and Break It, So Shall Thy Prayers Be Answered

The velocity of the liquefied landslide intensified as the two overarching side streets united. Arman hung on for dear life, for he knew if he were to slip back into the metallic stew he would certainly be crushed to death. Miraculously, the powder-blue bug continued to stay afloat, and Arman wasn't about to start questioning her paradoxical buoyancy. Contrary to the deafening roar that accompanied its pilgrimage inland, the superfluous mass of ocean appeared tame and docile, as it slithered back into its basin. The streets were eerily silent, with the exception of the grating symphony of creaks and groans emanating from the procession of wood and metal.

Arman poured down St. Peters Way, one of the two overarching streets that formed the two arms of the wishbone and eventually melded into the base of the bone, known as Serpents Cove. Sansar was clinging to life within the Pearly Gates, the northerly arm of the wishbone. Unbeknownst to them both, their destinies lay in the mercy of the current. The two sister streets would eventually empty into St. Peters Basin, the inferior outlet of the wishbone.

As the two streets collided, the variance of currents nearly hurled Arman off of his powder-blue perch. He clawed the roof, tooth and nail, despite utter exhaustion. Moments after Arman's debut, Sansar washed into the cove, desperately clinging to a fragment of the fresh piling he had navigated earlier. The confluence of debris and salt water snapped the distal ends of his salvation like a salted pretzel rod. As the two brothers washed into St. Peters Basin, the forward motion once again abated, as the sea wrestled the incline of the meandering landscape.

Amongst the litany of creaking and clanging melodies arose the most beautiful note Arman had ever heard. He lifted his weary head as the blood trickled down his chin, "Brother, is it you? Could it be?" He barely recognized the enfeebled, withered moans drifting up ever so slowly behind him, but there was something about them. It was immediately obvious, whoever it was that lay draped over the remainder of piling was in bad shape, but he was alive. As the muffled cries grew closer, a warm breeze passed by Arman's cheek and brushed the branches and reeds from the man's face, "My God! Is it you? Is it really you? Thank you, Lord! My prayers have been answered!"

Not only was he alive, but he had miraculously found his way within an arms length of his little brother. Arman broke down and cried like a little child, "Sansar, thank God!" The elder brother could barely lift his head due to extensive blood loss. Arman reached out his arm, "Take my hand, my brother." Sansar valiantly reached out his mangled limb. Arman, with every ounce of strength he could conjure, pulled his brother's almost lifeless body atop ol' powder blue. Arman immediately heaved his tee shirt over his head, despite his shattered elbow, and wrapped it around Sansar's missing digit, securing the ends around the exposed bone.

"My shoulder, it is surely broken," Sansar muttered in agony.

Arman took his brother's face in his hands and kissed both of his cheeks. He gently laid his head upon his chest and wept, "I did not think I should ever see you again."

Sansar laid his hand on Arman's cheek, "You are a sight for sore eyes, my little brother." A moment of silence elapsed as he gazed into Arman's welling eyes, "It looks like Mama's money was well spent after all." Their pathetic attempt at laughter was quickly overruled by pain and weakness.

Arman lifted his head and surveyed the surrounding debris, "I think we will be alright. I have been atop this majestic blue bug since the recession, and yet she still floats."

"That is good to hear, my little brother, but that is not what worries me."

"I do not understand," Arman said with a perplexed stare. Sansar mustered up just enough strength to lift his finger, and pointed into the distance.

All of the surrounding debris that had accompanied them in the relentless procession towards the sea was descending into the Sunflower Hill Mall's basement parking garage at a furious rate. It was a one-way ramp to the lower level: one-way down, and one-way up. They were now at the mercy of the current and everything it had collected, and ol' powder blue was being escorted, against her will, to an unescapable watery grave.

42

The Book of Memoirs

The creature's metamorphosis was now complete. No longer did it bare any resemblance to Mr. Wetherly's decomposing corpse. It was now completely translucent, vigilantly slithering back and forth, waiting for the pews to fill. Despite the terror resounding within the church walls, the creature remained silent. It reared its ugly head and methodically honed in on the glimmering electrical supply overlooking the altar. As it raised its translucent tail, it tauntingly grazed the metal frame of the outlet, making sure it was visible for all of the horrified congregation to see. With a single thrash of its angry barb, the tattered statue of Jesus, along with Pastor Connelly's impaled body, fell to the altar and shattered, like a porcelain doll, into a thousand pieces. I felt sick to my stomach and could feel the blackness begin to come over me as memories began to flood my darkening mind. Perhaps it was a defense mechanism to spare me from going into shock, or a diversion from the terrifying reality of what was to come. Whatever it was, it was working.

43

The Book of Memoirs: Christmas Eve - A Watched Pot Never Boils

"Christy, pass the biscuits, will you, sweetheart? And stop teasing your sister." I passed the biscuits over to Grandma, but not before sneaking one more for myself, of course.

"Christy," Mama chimed in, "eat your dinner, baby. It's gonna get cold."

"It's not cold, Mama, but your water is boiling over again."

"It can't be, Christy. Mommy turned the stove off." I shoveled a generous spoonful of sweet potato into my cheeks and nonchalantly repeated myself with perhaps a slight twinge of arrogance, "It's boiling ohhhhver." Mama brushed it off like she usually did and stood at the foot of the table to ask the annual rhetorical question, "Does anyone want any pie?" We all knew better than to refuse Mama's creations, which were constructed from scratch the night before, and a result of countless hours worth of tedious labor. Mama got up and excused herself, pridefully reveling in the glory of her precious pastries. "Stop kicking me!" Hailey huffed, as she stuffed her cheeks with stuffing. I laughed. When I looked up Mama was standing in the doorway, staring at the table like a deer in the headlights.

"What is it, Gwen?" Grandma asked inquisitively.

"Did you turn this water on, Christy?" Mama asked sternly.

"No, Mama," I said, still chewing my sweet potato.

"Then how did you know the water was boiling over?"

"I just knew, Mama," I said innocently.

Mama looked at me funny for a few moments and dismissed it, just like she always did, "I guess I thought I turned it off. Oh well, who wants pie!?"

44

The Little Blue Pill

Debris collided from every angle, every alleyway, swallowed whole by the gaping jaws of the monstrous subterranean parking garage, as it groaned and creaked with delight. Screams of steel and metal haunted the halls as they scraped the concrete on their descent to the underworld. The reverberating clangs and clamor echoed through the pharynx of the one-way tunnel, taunting the two men like circus music emanating from a sinister carnival ride. A ride on which the two men were destined to embark, whether they liked it or not.

The belching beast arched its neck and swallowed them up like a little blue pill. Their screams echoed off the walls of the concrete esophagus as they emptied into the bowels of the basement. The garage was already half full prior to the recession, optimistically speaking, of course, and Ol' blue collided with the collection of bile deep in the pit of the beast's filling stomach.

"Now I know how an after dinner mint feels," Sansar whimpered with a cynical tongue. Arman humored him with a courageous chuckle, "Yeah, take two and call me in the morning." The battered brothers did their best to don a brave face, but the reality of the situation weighed heavily, the reality that there was indeed, no conceivable way out.

45

The Book of Memoirs: Hailey's Second Birthday - Under Pressure

"Christy, we need some wipes for this spill! . . . Christy, we need some more forks! . . . Christy, fetch some more cake for the girls, will ya, honey!?" Hailey was getting all of Mama's attention, and I was getting none. So I plopped the cake down under their greedy little chins and stormed back into the kitchen. "Behave, Christy," Mama snapped sternly, yet calmly. "I have enough on my plate right now without tending to you as well." In a moment of selfish solitude, I conjured thoughts of how I could sabotage this unjust little tea party. I sulked and brainstormed until I was red in the face. But something funny happened. As I peeked through that doorway and eyeballed the pretentious little soiree, a moment of clarity ensued. I realized how much fun Hailey was having, and how happy she was. My guilty conscience prevailed over my childish self-pity, and I marched back into the dining room with wipes, forks, and a fresh batch of birthday cake, and apologized to Mama. She accepted with a loving smile and tended to the sugar-fueled little munchkins.

And that's when all hell broke loose. Suddenly the kitchen sounded like the Fourth of July, like gunshots going off. The sounds of laughter quickly turned to screams as Mama and Grandma whizzed by me and ran into the kitchen. There was a moment of sweet serenity that seemed to last an eternity, and then . . . wait for it . . . "Oh . . . my . . . God! . . . CHRISTY!!! . . . You get in here right now, young lady!" The green mile beckoned. I slowly opened the swinging door and stood there in disbelief. There was soda everywhere! Mama and Grandma stood, hands on hips, in a puddle of fructose and carbonation, as the corn syrup trickled down the walls and dripped from the ceiling. Mama didn't even ask for an explanation. She pointed a finger upstairs and said in a bridled voice,

"Get up to your room, now."

"But Mama, I didn't . . ."

"NOW!" And that was that. Mama was mad for almost a whole week. She didn't believe me, as usual. Maybe now she will believe me.

46

For Mama

Monstrous mounds of debris eclipsed the distant entrance, jamming the blue bug into the darkest corner of the filling deathtrap. Ol' blue was slowly but steadily ascending towards the ceiling. They both knew it was only a matter of time before the garage filled completely, entombing everything it had consumed. The two brothers shivered in solitude amidst the haunting chimes of scraping metal and rising water,

"All of this is because of us!" Arman chattered as he began to sob. "Forgive me, Father, for I have sinned."

"Don't be foolish, my brother," Sansar interjected. "It was just a matter of time before someone else unearthed that stupid book! We are all innocent, every single one of us. We did not ask for this existence. It was given to us without our consent. Would it be any different if our lives were granted by a so-called loving God? Or a maniacal genie? Either way, we have no say. Personally, I would have taken the maniacal genie over the sociopathic race, hell-bent on unconditional extermination, any day, but that's just me," Arman professed sarcastically, shivering from head to toe.

The realization that the ceiling was closing in with every passing second was too much for Arman to bear, "I don't want to die!" he cried. "Not like this! Knowing there is no heaven, no afterlife, no nothing!"

Sansar pulled his head into his arms and held him gently, "Arman, my little brother, you have always meant the world to me.

Although our time here may have been pointless and meaningless, we have been blessed to have had each other for as long as we did, and even more blessed to be together now. Love is the one thing we, as a race, have created, and the one thing they can never take away."

Arman laid his head upon his brother's chest and wept openly, "I love you, Sansar. You have always been my hero and always will be." Arman wiped his tears, and attempted to regain his composure as the garage creaked and moaned like a tortured soul, "Do you remember the story you told me about the girl who was trapped in the well?" Arman surveyed the bleakness of the filling tomb, shivering uncontrollably, "Now I know how she felt."

"Listen to me, Arman." Sansar whispered. "I never told you this before, but Mama always said you were her angel, literally. She said after our father left, you were the only reason she didn't take her own life. She knew I would have been ok because I was older, but she could never have left you. You saved her life! And you are my angel right now. And we both have some of Mama's strength in us, and we will go with dignity, just like Mama did. Can you do that? Can you be strong for Mama?"

Arman looked up at his brother's angelic face from the pit of his warm chest, laid his hand upon his cheek, and whispered meekly, "For Mama."

47

The Book of Memoirs:
The Chill of Skutters Lake

(And the memories kept coming, even the one's I so desperately tried to suppress . . .)

"Christy, lace up your skate, honey, you're gonna fall flat on your face!" Mama cried from the old wooden bench at the edge of the lake. "And keep an eye on your sister!" I could see Mama smiling and talking to Grandma through the steam of my breath. Skutters Lake froze most every winter back then, and Mama was always so happy to see us having the time of our lives. I always felt safe when she was watching.

The shiny steel blades scratched the surface of the lake like new diamonds. Oh, how I loved that sound. I was happy. All my friends were there, and so was Tommy McConnell, the boy I had a crush on since kindergarten. The oyster sky gazed down as her rolling grey clouds danced playfully across the ice. It was really quite beautiful. However, I couldn't stop staring at Tommy McConnel. He could barely stand on the ice, but my God, was he cute! I could tell he kinda liked me but was too shy to say anything. I glanced out toward the edge of the lake. Mama was busy debuting the new scarf she was working on for Hailey to Grandma. As I turned back, there was Tommy McConnel, sprawled out at my feet, lying flat on his back. "Are you Ok?" I asked reluctantly, brandishing a coy smile. I couldn't believe my mouth actually worked and formed a word, never mind a whole sentence. Tommy brushed himself off, smiled, and bashfully skated away. I almost melted.

When I snapped out of it, I realized Hailey was no longer by my side. She had somehow evaded everyone's radar and hobbled over to the far end of the lake. I could see her clinging to the *No Skating Beyond This Point* sign. It was the first time I had ever consciously felt the feelings . . . the premonitions. I thought I was having a panic attack or something. She was so far out and completely separated from the herd. My face flushed as I felt something warm run down my leg. I realized I had just wet myself, something I had never done before. And it wasn't because I was afraid, it was something bigger than that.

The bevy of blades scratching the ice soon became louder, unbearably so. I could hear the shivers of sheered ice, as they settled back onto the lake. The monotone rumble of discourse within my proximity became individually discernible, so much so that I could hear Mama boasting to Grandma 'bout how she saved a pretty penny on the wool at The Barnyard. As I discreetly glanced down at my leg, and surveyed the damage of my renal snafu, something from under the murky water emerged, and tapped at the ice underneath my feet. A ghostly figure appeared. I rubbed my eyes, thinking tears from the wind had obscured my vision. It was not the wind. Whatever it was alligator rolled onto its belly, and brushed the undercarriage of the ice. At first I thought it was a large air bubble, that is, until it made eye contact.

The ghostly image then laid what appeared to be a palm underneath my feet. A reaper-like translucent appendage pointed across the lake towards Hailey. In a split second it arced its protruding digit and tapped the frozen lake with the power of a hole-punch. The crack danced across the surface, evading all of the oblivious frolicking children. Its path was unmistakably clear. I screamed as loud as I could, "HAILEY!!!" The solitary bolt divided exponentially, inches before her, and enveloped the ice underneath her feet. A sickening shatter preceded a frigid splash, and she was gone, and so was my innocence.

She didn't even have time to scream. It was as if the lake itself had pulled her under. My heart pounded through my chest. I could hear Mama and Grandma screaming her name at the top of their lungs as the lavender scarf fell to the ground. Mr. Brody and the other parents scrambled onto the ice and scurried towards the gaping hole. She was nowhere to be found. "Oh my God!!!" a woman screamed from the center of the lake, "She's over here!!! She's over here!!!" Three men stumbled across the glazed surface. Two of the men fell to their knees once they saw the ghostly blonde silhouette floating underneath the leaden lake. Mr. Brody ran to his pickup at the water's edge and pulled out two shovels and a pick-axe from the tailgate. The three men frantically pounded the ice as her pale white stare peered through the frozen glass. I couldn't be sure if she was still alive or if it was just the current moving her arms against the ice. I think I may have been going into shock because I couldn't move, not a muscle. I thought I was going to die right there on that lake.

Just then Grandma whisked me off the ice. I watched Mama fall to her knees, gutturally screaming Hailey's name, from Grandma's shoulder, as she carried me to the car. Mama pounded on the ice with her bare hands, joining Mr. Brody and the men. The lake stained red as she and the men assaulted the thick ice in vain. The other parents grabbed jacks and crowbars from their trucks and joined them, painstakingly chipping away. Embers of ice filled the cold November air and rained down upon the lake like a fairy tale that had gone terribly wrong. Fifteen agonizing minutes had elapsed before Brody's pick-axe breached the icy tomb. Grandma's arm clenched my body as she cried out Hailey's name under her breath. I could feel her body shake as she wept. They pulled her out of the frigid depths and laid her little body upon the ice. Mama knelt over her, as the men tried to revive her. Grandma whispered her name over and over, as she pleaded with God not to take her. She began to pray out loud,

He who dwells in the shelter of the most high will rest in the shadow of the Almighty. I will say of the Lord, "He is my refuge and my fortress, My God, in whom I trust." Surely he will save you from the fowler's snare and from the deadly pestilence. He will cover you with his feathers, and under his wings you will find refuge, his faithfulness will be your shield and rampart.

You will not fear the terror of night, nor the arrow that flies by day, nor the pestilence that stalks in the darkness, nor the plague that destroys at midday.

But whoso shall offend one of these little ones which believe in me, it were better for him that a millstone were hanged about his neck, and that he were drowned in the depth of the sea.

As Grandma bargained with the Almighty, I watched the hole at the dark end of the lake close up upon itself. A cold wind blew across Skutters Lake as I felt Hailey's breath leave her. She lay limp and lifeless, draped over Mama's arm, like a ghost in a little white sweater. I felt the blackness come over me as Mama screamed into the wintery sky, and the chill of Skutters Lake was forever in my bones.

48

Tis the Blood of Thy Covenant
Thicker Than the Water of Thy Womb?

The exhausted blue beetle bobbed up and down, an arms length from the encroaching concrete canopy. The roof was closing in, as the recession ravaging the outside world was slowly clawing her way back into the sea. The rush of water inside the flickering deathtrap crescendoed, in unison with their pounding hearts. The fear of death had gripped Arman to the point of hyperventilation. Sansar, selflessly suppressing the reality of a godless death, interlocked fingers with his fearful brother and began to recite the prayer of impending doom,

> *The Lord is my shepherd; I shall not want.*
>
> *He maketh me to lie down in green pastures:*
>
> *he leadeth me beside the still waters.*
>
> *He restoreth my soul:*
>
> *he leadeth me in the paths of righteousness for his name's sake.*

Arman knew, deep in his heart as well, that the solace of a loving God no longer existed, yet the rhythm of his brother's voice comforted him, and he began to pray,

> *Yea, though I walk through the valley of the shadow of death,*
>
> *I will fear no evil: for thou art with me;*

thy rod and thy staff they comfort me.

Thou preparest a table before me in the presence of mine enemies:

thou anointest my head with oil;

my cup runneth over.

Surely goodness and mercy shall follow me all the days of my life:

and I will dwell in the house of the Lord for ever.

The rhythmic pentameter of their prayers turned to whimpering cries for mercy, as the invading ocean devoured the remaining nook of oxygenated real estate. A final breath, a final scream, and there was blackness. Only blackness. Mountains of debris devoured the daylight, and endless ocean flooded any surviving circuitry. The valiant pocket of air in ol' blue disappeared, and the heroic little beetle sank to the bottom like a blackening stone. The yearning for oxygen was far too great for their burning lungs as they sank deeper into the abyss. The water pried their jaws apart and invaded them like poison. The pain unlocked their fingers and the two brothers, once miraculously reunited, drifted apart and descended into the frigid underworld.

The four walls collaborated, reciting a eulogy of creaks and groans, to an otherwise empty reception, as the gulls cried mournfully atop their pensive pillars. A gold crucifix settled on the ocean floor beside their feet, and all was still. Peace was finally upon them, and flowed over them like a warm veil, dancing in the wind.

49

The Shiny Metal Box

The chill of Skutters Lake lashed my cheek with a wicked wind, and snapped me out of my disturbing little stroll down memory lane, and back into the hell that had infected our holy little church. The creature taunted the horrified prey entangled in its aqueous web, feinting and weaving its tail closer and closer to the power supply. Two shrill screams bellowed from the adjacent pew in front of us. It was Gladys Jones and another woman, trying in vain to stop Mr. Catalano, distraught from the loss of his beloved wife, from a suicidal walk of vengeance towards the creature. Mama gently lifted me from her shoulder and placed me atop the filling pew, "Christy, don't move baby!" She ran down the central aisle, and along with a few of the others, wrestled Mr. Catalano back onto the bench.

As the women struggled to restrain the grief stricken man, my solitude summoned a final flashback. It was a chilly November Sunday morning. We arrived early for mass upon our descent of the frosted hill. My nose was running, so Daddy escorted me to the church storage closet in search of a box of tissues. It was the very last memory I would have of him before he left for heaven.

"We gotta start home schoolin' you, little lady. Too many germs in them damn schools. Seems like you got a cold every other Sunday." I recalled the shiny metal box glistening above my head.

"Daddy? What's in the pretty metal box?" The box was set high upon the wall in the back of the storage closet.

120

"It's just a circuit breaker, baby. It turns off the power, along with the lights and stuff. Why so many questions, honey? Are you writing a book?"

I nodded playfully, "As a matter of fact, I am."

He grabbed my hand and pulled me along, "I should like to read this book of yours one day, but for now we need to get back to our seats before Mommy sends out the hounds."

I never completely understood what happened to Daddy. I was only four when he went to heaven. Daddy was a commercial fisherman and was gone quite a bit, sometimes days at a time. One night as I spied from the top of the bannister, I heard Mama talking to Grandma about it. Mama said the hull of *Hailey's Haven* split in two and no one survived the frigid Atlantic waters. Daddy named his boat after Hailey the day we sprinkled her ashes into the ocean. He told me that her memory kept him warm on those bitter nights at sea. Mama said there wasn't a cloud in the sky the day it happened; no one could explain it. Mama never spoke of it again, at least not in front of me. She handled it the best way she knew how, "Daddy had to go to heaven, sweetie. But we will see him again when the time comes. We must be patient." Not much of a consolation, but what else could a mother possibly say to a four-year-old little girl?

As I recalled the darkest hours of my life, I thought about how much I missed him, and how much I loved Mama. I also thought about that shiny metal box. As Mama and the other ladies wrestled Mr. Catalano to his seat, I snuck off towards the elusive storage closet. I evaded everyone's radar, including the distracted creature, preoccupied with processing the potential threat from the pews. The water was warm and strangely viscous. I tried my best not to make a sound as I slowly sloshed through the alien fluid. As I rounded the corner, the covert little cavern and her shiny metal box beckoned. It was as if nothing had changed, even the old wooden stool remained, cloaked in cobwebs, exactly as we left it.

The commotion from the pews echoed in my ear and I knew there wasn't much time. I started my ascent up the old rickety stool. It creaked in disapproval, as I tried to pretend I was lighter than I was. I prayed with all my might that I would not be heard. The stool teetered back and forth as I veered the summit. I could still see, from the corner of the hallway, the bronze statue of Jesus as it hung valiantly from the altar. That was all I could see. I continued to climb. My heart pounded so hard, I feared that it too, may be heard. A final step, and there I stood, face to face with the shiny metal box from my past. It wasn't as shiny as I remembered it to have been, for the dampness and the years had marred her once glowing complexion. Nevertheless, I had little time to ponder her aging attributes, as the old stool wrestled with the asymmetry of its bum leg. I braced myself as best I could, leaned against the wall, amongst the shelves of neglected nick nacks, and pulled at the metal housing to expose the circuitry. To my horror, the lackluster metal vault was rusted shut. I pulled again and again to no avail. The ailing stool wobbled precariously with each failed attempt. I stopped and listened for a brief moment, for silence was what I feared most. To my relief, the commotion from the nave continued to haunt the halls. I could hear Pastor Connelly chanting bible verses, his voice getting louder and more intense with each passage, as if he were trying to exorcise the demon,

The Lord is thy keeper: the Lord is thy shade upon thy right hand!!!

The sun shall not smite thee by day!!!!

Nor the moon by night!!!!!

The Lord shall preserve thee from all evil: he shall preserve thy soul!!!!!!

A dull thud preceded a collective gasp, and the words were suddenly silenced. As I glanced over from my shaking stool, I saw Pastor Connelly hit the wall with such force that the back of his skull wedged onto the bronze thorns upon Jesus' head. A bloodied limp body in a black gown now hung from the crucifix above the altar. I covered my mouth and whimpered into my hand as the blood ran down his face. I forced myself, with all my strength, not to look, and focused on the task at hand, for I knew there was little time.

I braced myself upon the shelves that loomed just above my chin, and surveyed the contents as I caught my breath. There were a handful of tools to my direct right that were miraculously within arms reach. I crossed my fingers and stretched as far as I could. A yellow flat-nosed screwdriver lingered a hair away from my burning, desperate outstretched fingers. The stool wobbled uncontrollably as I summoned every inch of strength I could muster, and leaned in for the kill. I clutched my hand over the taunting yellow handle, "Got cha!" I muttered under my breath. The very second I grabbed the handle, the top shelf collapsed upon itself. The metal and glass tenants clamored as they crumbled into the waiting ooze below my feet. My body froze solid; I couldn't breath. I listened for the commotion. There was nothing.

I heard Mama scream my name, "CHRISTY!!!" I panicked, for I knew the creature was privy. I pried at the aluminum casing as my hands shook uncontrollably. The rusted door swung open just as the screwdriver fell from my hands. That's when the dreaded silence turned into my worst nightmare. A long, wavering collective shriek echoed through the church, and reverberated through the dripping hallway. I will never forget it. The lights in the hall flickered and blew out over my head. It was too late! The church was black and the silence was upon me. I cried for Mama under my breath, but there would be no answer. I was alone . . . a seven-year-old little girl, sitting atop a creaking stool, in a dark flickering closet.

50

The Day Grandma Went to Heaven

"**G**randma! Grandma!"

"*Oh my goodness, you girls get bigger every time I see you. How was church, my angels?*"

"*We had to Jenny-flex every two minutes,*" I huffed rebelliously.

Grandma almost laughed her bifocals off the bridge of her nose, "You mean genuflect, sweetheart."

"*Why do we have to kneel, I mean Gen~u~flex all the time?*"

"*You are paying respect to the Lord, sweetheart.*"

"*Does he kneel to us? Does he respect us, Grandma?*"

"*Of course he does, sweetie.*"

"*I'm confused then, if God made us, who made him?*"

"*God was always here, sweetheart,*" *she replied in a soft comforting tone.*

"*Then how do we know we weren't always here?*" *I replied, unsatisfied with Grandma's infinite wisdom.*

"*Christy, you are too young to be concerning yourself with such things.*"

I looked at Grandma with a dead stare, "God made the lights flicker in church today, but Mama didn't believe me."

Grandma paused for a moment, "That's funny, come to think of it, he made the lights flicker over here too."

Mama was never the same after we lost Grandma that Sunday morning. I miss her every single day. Grandma and I had a very special bond. I think she saw something in me that Mama didn't. She gave credence to my so-called imaginative stories. Mama liked to chalk them up to my overactive seven-year-old imagination, God bless her soul. But Grandma listened. She always listened. I remember just before she died, I told Mama that the faucets in the bathroom were dripping more than they usually did, especially the bathtub, "It's alright, Christy," she said. "A little water never hurt anyone." I wish she had listened.

Mama found Grandma in the tub that Sunday morning just before church. I never saw her, but I heard Mama crying, telling the police she was only in there for a few minutes. Mama insisted she couldn't have fallen asleep. There was talk of ligature markings on her wrists and ankles, yet no restraints were ever found. She said the water was dripping from the ceiling, and that's when she knew something was wrong. I heard Mama crying in the bathroom, and ran upstairs, but she closed the door and quickly whisked me away. I wept as the water followed us down the stairwell, for I already knew what had happened.

Mama had just lost Daddy, and now Grandma was gone. I used to think that God must have really loved our family because he kept taking them to heaven. The next morning I tried not to look in the bathroom. But I did. The water had stopped dripping.

51

The Chosen One

My heart grieved for Mama, but my thoughts were now consumed by the ghost in the darkness. I felt the creature's presence in the shadows, and for all I knew the fluid beneath my feet still crawled with lethal voltage. I whimpered under my breath, and with a shaking hand, disengaged the main circuit breaker. God knows how old that fuse box was, or if it even worked. I prayed that the power was off. I also prayed for Mama to take me in her arms and carry me home, but I knew in my heart she was gone. Everyone was gone. The forsaken house of God staggered in darkness and silence. Droplets of rain fell like tears through the rafters and echoed through the moonlit hallway, as a lonely wind howled beyond the church walls.

I wondered about the outside world and what remained. I decided to take my chances, and inched my way down the trembling wooden antique, poking and prodding my way through the darkness. I reached out my trembling leg, crossed my fingers, and braced myself for contact with the precarious ooze. That's when I felt the presence upon me. My ankles immediately buckled, and I fell face first into the putrid pool. To my relief, I was still alive. As I lay shivering in the shallows, I felt something coil around my legs. It lifted me out of the fluid, feet first, and proceeded to bind my arms. It swung me effortlessly into the air and dangled me, a hair's breadth from the ceiling. I could not see it, but felt its ugly presence inches from my face. Even worse, I smelled its foul stench as it studied me from every angle. I screamed, and its tail tightened painfully around my throat. That was the last thing I remembered before the blackness stole my breath and bestilled my beating heart.

52

The Aftermath

And so it was . . . The great floods began to recede, and the wind drew its last breath upon the ravaged plains. The cloak of death lifted, and revealed its ugly reign. The extermination was complete. Only the scavengers remained. Bodies littered every corner of the globe, the stench of death corroded the air, and the crow feasted heartily. Dark clouds scoured the land like vultures, and the Earth lay barren and still, once again. Life as we knew it ceased to exist . . . or did it?

53

With Great Rain Comes Pretty Flowers

"No one ever believes a child," Christine etched painfully into her journal. A chronic trembling in her right hand made her writings difficult to decipher, almost as difficult as the unspeakable text itself. As she wrestled the tremors, she entered yet another disturbing memory, *"The lights flickered again in church today, Grandma. And Jesus was sad. You know how I know? A tear rolled down his cheek. Maybe all those candles made him sad. Maybe he too, knew what was to come. Do you think so, Grandma?"* She laid the pencil upon her journal and cradled her face in her hands. As she conjured up the past, a silent soliloquy haunted her weary thoughts,

Looking back now, there were so many signs: the flickering lights, the leaky faucets, the incessant barking, Hailey's second birthday, the omnipresent sentry clouds . . . so many signs. And the birds! The one thing I remembered about Sunday morning mass was the birds, and how they were always singing their songs. There were no songs, only the atonal chants of pastor Connelly and the eerie call and response of the congregation. So many signs, I wish I could have seen it. But even if I had, there was nothing I could have done. At least that's what I keep telling myself.

It has been thirteen years to the day, since the unspeakable events, yet the birds sing their song once again. I have two beautiful little girls of my own, and a lovely man who I have come to love, although sometimes, I must confess, I still wish it was the boy from the lake. But I suppose fairytales are nothing more than fairytales.

I'm not sure why they chose us, why they chose any of us. Word has it that the chosen ones were methodically and strategically selected across the globe. It is said that we are all gifted, harbingers of things to come. This is all I know. Despite the selective cleansing, the planet is once again beginning to flourish. The bodies have been reduced to dust, and the stench lifted. The flowers bloom, and the plains prosper with new soil. Both the raven and dove sing their song, and the chants of children linger once again. But nothing can ever be the same. We are nothing more than prisoners to a sadistic God. The hardest part of it all is the burden of silence we all must bare, for if any one of us should ever speak of the unthinkable events, the children shall surely perish.

I write this journal for my own sanity, in hopes that no one will ever find it. I guess Daddy was right, I was writing a book: *The Greatest Story Never Told*, I guess you could say. Life is different now, very different, and my daughters are the center of my world. Every now and then the darkness creeps back into my thoughts, and in light of the unforeseen events, I sometimes wish I had never conceived, and for that I am truly ashamed. I would ask for forgiveness but there is no one to grant it. I realize I shouldn't blame myself, for the fear of death was my impetus, but I still do. You see, our mates were predetermined, and we were forced to procreate upon menstruation. Destiny and Grace will never know why they are here. At least they will never know the truth. Maybe that's the way it should have been from the beginning. Maybe we are all better off not knowing. What we don't know can't hurt us, right? Don't get me wrong, they will learn of the Good Book and abide by it, just as all the others shall, but we, the chosen ones, will always know the truth. I sometimes think that if we could just find comfort in each other, we wouldn't have to reach for some ludicrous explanation for our existence. I think back to when I was a little girl myself. I'll admit the idea of heaven and a loving, omniscient God comforted me. But I always felt as though I were clinging to a ghost. Truth be told, Mama's love was my savior. She was real. And so was Grandma and Hailey, and even Daddy for a little while. It's all around us! Love thy brother, that's all we can do. That's all any of us can do now.

A warm wind drew its breath upon the restless blinds as the morning rain gently tapped upon the window. The raven did crow and the dove did coo. And the lavender and Jerusalem sage did bloom. A solitary tear stained the forbidden page as Christine laid her weary pencil to rest. The clock on the wall chimed eleven. She yelled up into the stairwell,

"C'mon, girls! We're gonna be late for church!"

"We know, Mama. We know," they whispered . . . from directly behind her.